ABOUT FACE

AN EROTIC NOVELLA

CRISTINA GEERTSEN

About Face

tellwell

Tellwell Talent
www.tellwell.ca

ISBN
978-1-77370-731-0 (Hardcover)
978-1-77370-730-3 (Paperback)
978-1-77370-732-7 (eBook)

You can't just play around the edges...

For M.P.M.

Prelude

I have a story to tell, it's time. I am an old woman now, but there are no regrets. As you read you might be surprised. Surprised that I do not regret, that I can now move on.

Forgive? Well, that is more difficult. Perhaps the one I need to forgive the most is myself.

But I shall let you be the judge. to judge who is noble and who is wanting, and to weigh my characters' moral worth … a fitting quest, as I was studying the ancient Egyptians, and the main job for Osiris, the god of the underworld, was to put the soul of the dead on the scale to decide their fate in the Afterlife.

So…what of the fates of my cast?

Isabella again stood across from his Hampstead house, shielded by the trees. Trees that were much taller now. And this time it was morning, not twilight as she remembered. There had been a deep yearning, an unstoppable compulsion to lurk again right here, with a chance to see Joshua again. The flight from NYC had been long and uncomfortable. Her aching back and arthritic knee had added to her discomfort. But she had rejoiced in the self-indulgence of her reminiscing, the images from a distant past flashing again before her mind's eye. A great distraction from an arduous journey.

A grey-haired figure walked haltingly through the iron gate and awkwardly navigated the steps to the front door, lifting the wheeled walker with each step. Grappling for keys from her bag, the bent woman took time to find the lock with her shaking hand. And just as the door opened Isabella gasped, realizing just then that she was looking at Freddie, a Freddie thirty years on.

We have all aged, Isabella muttered under her breath, transfixed as she observed the changes in her old lover, that lover who had been so very demanding and manipulative. Hard to believe the power she had once held. Isabella winced as she had another flash of memory, a vivid picture of the three of them entwined in vibrant shawls, reclining on tasselled cushions, with the debris of their excessive feast of wine and gourmet foods strewn all around them on the floor of Joshua's studio. He had just finished another painting of her, his 'Bella' as Joshua had called her. The painting was the last of the series, all to be hung in the exhibition in Paris. They were celebrating, all together this time. Unusual for them, as normally it was Joshua and Isabella, with Freddie content to watch from a curtained alcove in the corner.

Isabella recalled how the tension had risen during that day. The day which was to be the final one for the trio. There had been the agreement that they would live as a ménage à trois to assist Joshua in his painting. He had implored Isabella to move in to be his inspiration. The completion of the collection had been delayed when she had been travelling from Cambridge, still trying to balance time on her post-doctoral research work and sitting as Joshua's model. Eventually she conceded, agreeing to give him a month, fully aware what it would mean for the complex intimacy that surrounded the three of them. Freddie had been insistent with Joshua. Isabella discovered later that Freddie had pushed a hard bargain. She would only continue to bankroll his painting if Isabella was available to her.

So, a pawn in a selfish game of competing egos? Just a degraded object at the whim of the sparring marital duo? No, Isabella was right in there, enjoying their adoration, their fixation and the, yes, loving care that came from them both.

But she was getting ahead of herself. It was all running in her head way too fast to really revel in the details. Isabella paused in the stream of seemingly unstoppable memories. She did not want to stand here much longer in the chill air. Time to move. Her breath caught at the base of her throat. Her legs shook and her knees felt weak. Now the initial shock of seeing Freddie was over, the buildup of adrenalin needed to brace her for this vigil was receding. She hesitated, feeling the physical power of the resistance in her body as she weighed her options. Forward to knock on that door? Or retreat? She sighed, a heavy heave to her shoulders and a misty bloom to her exhaling breath. Such powerful memories. Such an extraordinary part of a life well lived. No regrets. And there was really no need to re-connect. To bring the past forward. Isabella decided no to the door.

He was waiting in the car. He would be wondering. It was time now to tell the whole story. A story long overdue, and he has been patient long enough.

Ms Isabella, Classics scholar
St John's College
Cambridge

Hampstead, London N8
3rd March

To the lovely Isabella,

This letter must find you. I don't even know your full name. Or what position you have at the college. It is imperative that I see you again!

Our meeting on the train has left me feeling adrift, restless. We left each other without exchanging numbers, or a plan. It was too abrupt. There is so much to explain. But can that wait?

I want you. My mind wants you. My body stirs when I think of you. I want to find you again – need to find you again. I keep thinking about your eyes, your skin, and that amazing hair – burnished is the best word, I think. I wonder about your body, your breasts, your belly. I imagine your curves, your warmth, luscious, succulent, encompassing me. I feel the sensations of being inside you, yes, fucking you in all kinds of ways, and then lying beside you and then making love to you – a very different thing – I want to show you the difference. I remember your tongue in your beautiful mouth, how it moved when you talked; I want to kiss that mouth, suck that tongue, take it right down inside my throat. I want to see what you would do with that tongue, where you would lick, suck, kiss.

I pictured you sitting opposite me on the train, but all I could see of your body was your magnificent head and face and that long, long neck. Oh ... I have to imagine the rest and when I do ... I am so aroused just writing this. You are my inspiration. I have this thought – no, more a feeling. My life is like being in a drought – so long without painting. But maybe now the drought is about to break. This is because of you.

Will you let me paint you? Please (I NEVER say please! But this time I shall) ... Will you come?

My studio is at my home in Hampstead – just near the tube station. The week of April 4 I shall be here alone. Any day that week I shall be working here – or at least hoping to work. I have tried to paint you since we met, but your image fades. It is impossible without you here, in front of me, for me to focus on. I need that.

Please come,
Joshua

The letter stood stiff in her hand. How much time had gone by? How many students had pushed past her in the mailroom?

"Isa … Isa ..." An insistent voice broke into her reverie. "What's wrong? What's happened? Is it that letter? You have gone quite white …

"Oh, Simon. No, it's okay, thanks. Just a bit of a shock, someone I met on the ... um at that conference a month or so ago …"

"Wow, you look dreadful. Shall I help you back to your room? Or we could go out later, a walk, or a drink?" Simon's warm tone expressed his concern as he looked closely into Isabella's face, trying to catch her averted eyes. She had cancelled their last few opportunities to meet up. And she had been away a lot recently. And now, she seemed so distant, distracted.

"No, I… I think I'll just go up now and…" Isabella's voice trailed off as she stumbled away, oblivious to Simon's caring, so caught up with what she held in her hand. Isabella felt that familiar weakness in her chest, that fluttering which came with excitement. Her hand shook as she folded the letter and put it away in her shoulder bag.

She felt dizzy, the room began to spin, and faces were ablur. She walked drunkenly out into the pale sunlight of a wintry March morning, breathing deeply, the misty air catching in her throat. The early fog was just rising, and the distinctive Tudor lines of the College roof were just revealing themselves.

So, he had found her after all.

CHAPTER ONE

She first noticed him in the queue at the ticket booth at Kings Cross. Standing behind him, there was something about his clothing – that jacket – velvet, brown, soft, and very well loved given the wear on the sleeves. And that silk scarf with its pattern. What was it? Paisley. Yes, a pattern from a former era.

She caught the faint smell of him as he stood in front of her. He moved aside to let someone pass. His fedora slouched over his eyes. The waistcoat too – cream, embossed like brocade. A musty odour, a little like mothballs. With an undernote of spice, musk. That caught her attention, her mouse brain was always so tuned in to smell. What did he do? Who was he? Was he in costume? Or was he just a bit eccentric? It was as if he were someone from a former time. An early Victorian gentleman. But, oh so very attractive! No time, however, she recalled, to indulge in the rather surprising feelings he sparked as the train was being called.

It was her turn to purchase her ticket. Then the rush to get on the train and find a seat facing backwards, the way she always liked. There was something about seeing where you have been all over again. So you didn't have to let the past go too soon. She loved the past. It was her addiction. Remembering.

She closed her eyes as the train left the station. She went over the material she had presented at that morning's seminar. More of the past – the ancient past. She was looking for corroborating evidence about Cleopatra before she became Queen of the Nile. This was Isabella's particular quest now.

Aware of a presence, she opened her eyes. He was right there, looking at her. Gazing right into her eyes! Had she dropped off to sleep for a moment? Had he willed her awake?

She became aware of his smell again, stirring her. Was she giving off an odour herself? Pheromones. Those early messages which send out signals of interest. Of availability. Way before words. Way before social conventions get involved and get in the way. Back to the cave, basic instinct, primal messages.

He sat very still as if drinking her in, his gaze travelled over her face and hair and down to her chest and hands. He came back to meet her eyes. He smiled. The smile crept up his face and lit up his eyes. Blue grey. The colour of smoke. There were crinkles at the corners of his eyes and mouth. Bare headed now, his tousled hair, brown, dusted with grey, curled against his collar.

Her breath caught as their eyes met. Her throat began to burn. She licked her suddenly parched lips and swallowed. His smile widened further, as if knowing his effect on her. She returned the scrutiny. Her turn to look him up and down.

The waistcoat was flamboyant, expressive. An actor? Artistic at the very least. Yes, that was it! She glanced at his hands. Long, thin fingers but strong, well-muscled hands. Hands with strength. A pianist perhaps, certainly a musician. But his hands were restless in his lap, repeatedly clenching then relaxing. She imagined those fingers caressing the neck of a violin or cello or playing a grand piano. Sensitive, flexible hands that had history. Hands that could sense without words. She could almost feel them on her neck, his fingers exploring behind her ears and along her hair line. Expert hands. Hands that could… Hmm, her mind was moving into that a bit too interested territory. He certainly would fall into a category of sexy. Ticks some boxes. Flushing, she cleared her throat and broke his gaze by looking out the window.

He spoke. A warm, low tone, with a touch of amusement. "Hello."

"Oh, hello," she said, "I must have dozed off."

"I have been watching you. Willing you to open your eyes. I was guessing their colour. I was right. They are a dark turquoise green. Like deep pools. Do they change colour like the sea changes with nature's moods?"

Taken aback by his directness, a demand for intimacy she was not yet willing to grant, Isabella responded lightly, "Well, I suppose I could say that you're wrong, and they're just coloured contact lenses, but I admit they're all me."

He smiled again, even wider this time. "Hey, I like your spirit. You must be used to strangers talking to you on trains."

"Strange men, yes," Isabella said with emphasis.

His laugh was an abrupt bark "Ha! Okay then, can we start over? I concede I am a little different, but hopefully not strange. My name is Joshua."

"Isabella."

It turned out she was wrong. He was not a musician but a painter. She felt caught, intrigued. Her fascination with him began.

"Oh, what kind of painter? Not houses, surely?"

She had fully woken up now, her brain clear, prepared for any more come-on lines.

"Not exactly … portraits mainly. But I haven't done any for a while. I have lost my inspiration. I am looking for a muse." He glanced sideways at her as he said this, a quite solemn expression around his mouth. A tensing of his jaw. He turned to look directly at her again, biting his bottom lip.

Isabella raised an eyebrow and opted to change the subject. "So the purpose for your trip to Cambridge? Are you going home?"

"No, I live in London, but I am doing some work for the Fitzwilliam. They want to bring in an exhibition from Paris and I am helping them negotiate the terms."

"Ah, Paris. Contemporary paintings?"

"No, Impressionists".

"Some of my very favourite pieces are in that period." Isabella suddenly felt self-conscious about her appearance, her hair likely windblown from that rush to get to the station and there had been no time to check her lipstick. She hadn't even thought of that until now.

"Is that right? Are you a student of art?"

"In a way I suppose, but much, much earlier than the Impressionists," she hedged.

Her indirect response focused his attention. He leaned forward watching her eyes and mouth as she spoke. Isabella explained that she was doing research in Classics at the University. She was a visiting Fellow from the States. Responding to his insistent questions, before she knew it, she had disclosed a lot about her project, even her secret desire to discover details about the early sexual life of Cleopatra, going back into her childhood and adolescence and her early relationships.

"Well, well, that sounds fascinating, but how do you get your material?" Joshua gazed at her even more intently as she began speaking animatedly about her work. He must really be interested. She felt flattered.

"That's the difficulty. There are so few primary sources. But I'm hopeful that there will be some evidence. And from that I can do some extrapolating.

A little educated speculation here, a little deduction there. Really, I can theorize all sorts of things."

Joshua grinned. "Hmm, you are just like me … into fantasy. Quite the voyeur. I think you'll just make it all up and then make out that it's legitimate academic work!"

Isabella lifted her chin. He was clearly teasing her. And the words didn't have quite the sting they might have had coming from someone else, like a colleague.

The train pulled into the station, and she was conscious of a tug of disappointment.

They parted in the train carriage amidst the flurry of activity, fellow passengers gathering their coats and hats and other belongings. On the platform, she looked back and saw his hat above the other heads, the brim turned away.

The disappointment was there again, emptiness in her gut, desire creeping into her loins to have more, know more. She had not felt that sensation for a long time, and it had been to her peril. She also felt that old urge to get away, to run. To allow all of it to belong just to the journey. To let the experience remain perfect in her memory, untarnished by what might come after. There was something between them. She felt it running through her body like an electric current. But she really knew nothing about him. For all she knew, he might be married. He might just have been whiling his time away on a train, flirting with a stranger. Perhaps he didn't feel this strange pull, this shiver that coursed her blood.

And she, was she just flirting as well? What was all this surge of feeling about? Did she not have a nice steady friend in Simon, back at college, who was clearly wanting to take things further. But did Simon trigger this longing, this fascination that was such a draw?

Joshua turned and their eyes met. She stilled, weak-kneed, but then was caught up with the crowd moving into the station. She shook her head as she was swept away. It was just a chance meeting. A meeting that was now over.

Almost at the gate, she realized she had left her umbrella behind. It was the one she had bought in Florence on a whim, with a crazy pattern on the fabric. When she opened it, there was Botticelli's Venus for all to see, emerging from her seashell. Yes, that umbrella always attracted stares, a few smiles. She didn't want to lose it. Swivelling, she walked fast, fighting against the flow of people.

Just as she reached the right part of the train, she noticed him. Joshua was standing on the carriage step, looking across the crowd.

He raised his hat with one hand. "Hello again, you left something."

The world stood still. She looked into his face. It was blurring around the edges. The crowd moved in slow motion in her peripheral vision. He brought his arm forward, her umbrella in his hand. How did he know it was hers? Had he known she would return for it? Her mouth opened and closed again. She stood before him speechless, jostled by the crowd.

He was smiling. "Come on."

He took her arm and walked with her to the barrier. Outside on the pavement, she pulled herself together. The air there was fresh; a cold wind blowing, and rain on the way. Joshua asked what college she was at, and she told him. She had a vivid memory of him bending towards her, about to ask her more when,

"Hey! Hey, Joshua, over here!" A strident shout from across the street. Joshua's head whipped around, a pallor edging across his cheek.

"Wha-at? What are you doing here?" Joshua suddenly dropped her arm and moved away, angling towards the harsh voice several metres away.

"Surprise!" The voice pitched louder over the wind. "I thought I'd come to…" the rest was lost in a rush of buses and shouting students on bicycles clattering past. Isabella moved away, glancing behind. Her last image of Joshua was of him dodging the traffic as he weaved across to a tall figure who stood rigid against the wind.

CHAPTER TWO

A black raincoat flapped, and black eyes smouldered beneath a low hat brim as the figure glared at the beautiful auburn-haired woman who opened an umbrella with an image of Venus. The eyes followed the umbrella as it quickly disappeared in the distance, just as the rain began.

They travelled back to London together the next day. Joshua had had his morning meetings about the upcoming exhibition, and Freddie was keen to show interest. An interest in what he was doing, the painting choices, the guest list, all of that. An interest that had been very lacking recently. She had become bored. She had stopped asking. And he had stopped sharing.

But not now. She felt the stirring of curiosity, of intrigue. Mmm…the cat's away and the mouse finds a very scrumptious piece of cheese on the train.

She wanted to surprise him. And yes, it had been quite the surprise. Joshua appeared to have to shake himself to get his brain back into this reality. The reality of the two of them, the old marrieds.

"So, now we are all matey here, tell me about the redhead who stood beside you on the pavement at the station yesterday." Freddie noted the ashen expression on Joshua's face as she poured another glass of wine.

"What have you been up to? I go up to the country and it sure didn't take you long! Must be something…all the colour is draining from your face!"

"Wh..at wh..at. Who?" blustered Joshua, "there you go, jumping to conclusions! For God's sake. She was just someone I met on the train. I don't even know her name."

They went on at each other like that for a while. Just like old times. Freddie interrogating, Joshua dodging, minimizing. The usual dance, with well-known choreography. But Freddie suspected, given the amount of energy and emphasis Joshua was putting into the denials, that something was up. If not up yet, it soon would be.

Her eyes gleamed. She almost licked her lips. "But better not be too obvious, too keen," she thought to herself.

Isabella found her bicycle, all tangled up with the others left that morning by students in a rush to catch their train. She felt lightheaded. Dizzy. Her lips were dry, and she felt thirsty, but not for water. She wanted more time with him. More information. More talk.

Why was that? What was it about him that had captured her? This man called Joshua.

And who was that person at the station? Hard to be completely sure in the gloom. But yes, her best hunch was a woman. Who was she to him? Colleague? Sister? No, probably wife, given that he had paled with the sudden shock of seeing her there. Well, Isabella had been there before, attracted to married men.

It had been a while though. She had pushed all that into the past. For more time than she would care to admit, she had focused on work and life quite separate from love and lust entanglements. Those always had ended in rejection and pain. These days, surrounded by all these smart, young students, it was rare that anyone gave her a second glance.

"Too old methinks." She mused to herself.

She wheeled her bike through the mid-afternoon traffic. The rain had stopped for now. The road was glistening. It was already getting dark, the sun obscured by dank fog. Lights from all manner of vehicles dazzled her. College students and youngsters in school uniforms muddled between office workers running for trains to create a mass confusion of bodies, wheels, damp coats and urgent faces in front of the station. There were too many people to be contained on the footpath; their numbers swelled into the road. Blaring horns and pealing bicycle bells brought her back to the present and she realized that she was disoriented, at risk of colliding with someone else and injuring herself. She shook her head to clear it from that cotton wooliness and concentrated on her route home.

Eventually making it back to her room in College, she stopped short at the door. She hadn't given him her last name!

A large part of her knowing that she should not, she nonetheless heard that inner voice wonder... "Will he try and find me?"

CHAPTER THREE

St John's College, March 15

Dear Joshua,

Yes, you did find me. I am at a loss as to what to say to you. In some ways our chance meeting seems like a lifetime ago. In others, it is as if it were yesterday. In honesty, my thoughts of you had receded. But with your letter it has all come flooding back.

Your explicit words leave me breathless. Your descriptions make me hot, sweaty, dizzy. Someone saw me read your letter and said I went quite white ... It is rare that I receive such lust through the mail. I am surprised with myself that I did not just tear it up, and here I am replying! And then there is the very obvious issue of how we parted. Someone called your name- who was it?

I do get up to London with my work from time to time. I have a seminar in the Gower St area with the University of London. I also need to use sources at the British Museum. I don't know about a painting ... I don't think I have the time for all that sitting around. We could talk about it some more I suppose. Maybe over coffee. But I do want an honest explanation about who met you.

Isabella

Isabella admired herself in the mirror as she dressed. She stood naked, reflecting on what she was doing, what might happen, and what he might see. How would he see her?

Her breasts were her favourite body part. Full and rounded, with responsive, pink nipples. They were not the perky peach shapes from her younger years; however, they had continued to serve her well. They'd been admired by many, and always satisfyingly sensitive when it came to lovemaking.

Isabella caressed them, rubbing both hands around and around, enjoying the warmth of her flesh. She had brushed her long hair smooth and then shaken her head to create the wavy, tousled effect she liked. Bed head. It shone in shades of russet and gold in the sunlight that filtered through the curtains into her room. Light strands of grey were blended in. She loved the colour. It suggested wisdom and the benefits of maturity.

She gazed at the rest of her body. Were the workouts in the college gym working? Her belly told the secret of her years more than anywhere else, but she didn't really mind; it could tell lots of stories. It was soft to the touch and very sensitive, especially on the edges of the pubic bones and across her womb. Her thigh muscles were long and lean. Strong.

With her fingertips, she brushed the tendrils of dark hair that lay between them, still damp from her shower. They too glowed with red and gold lights in a neat, small triangle, clipped into a vee which pointed the way to wondrous delights below. Her fingers searched with more purpose, untangling the hairs, and discovering the moisture beneath. With her thumb and middle finger, she parted the lips, and her forefinger touched the tip of her clitoris as it sprang to life. It was warm and still a little soft, but she knew that it would harden in an instant if she kept up the pressure just a little more. She looked up at her face, her eyes were dreamy, smoky, and her lips were stretched in a secret smile.

"I wonder how many middle aged, female fellows at this highly respectable university could be seen masturbating in front of a mirror on this very sunny spring morning?" she asked herself aloud.

It was probably more than one would imagine. Behind all those formal towers and traditional mullioned windows, they were all at it. Students, dons, secretaries, the college fellows, the dean, the master of the college. All of them! And more besides! The butcher, the baker, the candlestick maker. She laughed.

Her mood shifted. The humour of the moment briefly reduced the desperate urgency to continue her quest to seek one of the violent climaxes that had so often wracked her body lately. Thoughts of Joshua, his letters, their imminent meeting, were all working her into a frenzy, increasing the frequency and intensity of her frigging. She often craved it as she rode her bicycle to class, or when drenched in sweat, her skin gleaming and oily with moisture from a workout. She'd return to her room and picture their meeting and what might follow until she climaxed in convulsive shaking. Her cunt turned to hot liquid. On each occasion, her usual one or two orgasms were insufficient to satiate this new thirst.

Steadying her breathing, Isabella touched her fingers to the letter on the dresser before meeting her eyes in the mirror.

Hampstead, London N8
27th March

Lovely Isabella,

I shall see you next week. I can't wait. I want us to soar to great heights. You seem to be hesitant. I can understand that. Yes, we have just met. And yes, I have some things to explain to you. I do understand. All that in time.

Sometimes you just know when you are around something great. You are that for me. I just know it. I want to look at you. To paint you. And while I paint you, I want you to talk to me. To tell me all about your life, your loves, your work. What turns you on. What turns you off. I want you to describe in minute detail how you would like me to make love to you. I would love to hear you talk. People don't talk enough when they have sex. Especially men. I know women want men to talk. They want to know what is in our heads. It turns me on.

As I write this I look out at the park. The wind is blowing the trees – a warm spring wind. The snowdrops are finished, except in the dark, wet places. There are crocuses and daffodils coming through. It makes me think of you – dark and wet, mysterious. I want to explore your body. To get to know it inch by inch. All the crevices and mounds and valleys and clefts. I want to worship your body. I want to kiss and lick you with the tip of my tongue. To go on a journey from your toes to your eyes, and touch all the delicious parts of you in between.

My cock is hard, hot, wet ... it is bursting through my pants. I can touch it through my pocket. I want to see your eyes as I touch myself. I want to see you touch yourself, play with yourself. Caress, stroke, kiss, lick, suck. Let us watch one another and learn all the ways we each reach our climax.

Let me tell you a story. This has been keeping me going until I see you. We meet. We know at once that we are excited, aroused. We do not speak. We sit and look. I take in your face and eyes and hair, comparing these things with my memories of you. Our fingers touch and our hands clasp on the tabletop. Your fingernail begins a slow, rhythmic, circling caress of my fingertips. One by one. It is so sensuous, so erotic. You move to the side of my hand, and then over the top of it with light, circling, tickling touches. My hand turns over. My palm is more sensitive than the back of my hand. Your circling fingertip traces the texture and lines in my palm. It drives me wild. I am already hard. Wanting you. Wanting things to go much faster. For us to be alone. To kiss and hold you. Most of all to crawl up inside you and feel the snug, hot texture of you. The wetness of your cunt, the soft folds sucking me down deep into you.

But I must wait. We are still at the table. At the very beginning. I don't want to miss anything. You look up at me with a teasing expression – I wonder what you're going to say?

J.

CHAPTER FOUR

As Isabella crossed the road to the National Portrait Gallery, a familiar sensation overtook her. That quickening, of pulse and breath, the dampness between her thighs, a catch at the base of her throat. Her breasts swelled and pushed against the silk of her shirt and her nipples hardened as they brushed against the lacy fabric of her bra. It was her best black bra, a new one in fact … She liked the way it pushed her breasts together, creating deep cleavage with a mound of warm flesh over the cups.

The imposing façade of the art gallery rose up before her, the columns standing sentinel in the wintry noon sun. She approached the side entrance. He would be inside, upstairs, waiting for her. She adjusted her coat collar, pausing to retie her scarf. She caught sight of her reflection in the glass of the revolving doors. A tall brunette, auburn hair streaming out behind her in the breeze, wearing high boots, a black raincoat, and a multi-coloured silk scarf, striding forward with a confident air, and with that secret smile which had caused several passersby to look more than once.

He was not upstairs. He was right there in the foyer waiting for her. He looked just the same. Brown hair curled at the nape of his neck. Clean-shaven. Creases in his cheeks at the beginning of his grin. In the part gloom of the foyer, she could not see the special quality of the grey of his eyes; but she knew it was there, even though she had only met him once. Those eyes were seared on her brain. She could read the twinkling pleasure in his face as he strode forward to meet her.

"You are so beautiful. Glowing. Radiant. You have an aura. It is blue and pearly white. It is shimmering all around the edges."

She laughed at his whimsy. "Hi ..." Her voice sounded small, shy even, echoing in the big hall. "Nice to see you too."

"I want to see your face when we arrive upstairs. So, I just hung around down here. Let's go up."

They moved together to the lift. Once inside it, they were alone. Joshua moved towards her. He inhaled her scent as his lips and nose brushed, so very gently, the sensitive skin just beneath her chin and up towards her ear. Not a real kiss, a mere caress – how butterflies would kiss, little more than his breath on her skin. The quivering in her chest started up again. Her mouth went dry, then wet with the saliva that paralleled the jolt of arousal between her legs. She opened her mouth to speak but could not. She became breathless, panting, light-headed. She turned her head willingly, mutely asking for more, wanting it, wanting him already.

The lift doors opened, and the mood was broken. There was a clamour of voices, dishes clattering, bodies moving back and forth in her peripheral vision. She breathed in – she could detect garlic, basil. The familiar everyday smells and sounds grounded her.

They stepped out of the lift, Joshua's rueful grin bringing further colour to her cheeks.

She looked about. "Wow!"

There beyond the windows of the restaurant was all of London spread out before her – the rooftops of the National Gallery, then on to Trafalgar Square, with Nelson's back turned towards her. The Houses of Parliament and Big Ben stood in the distance. She caught just a glimpse of the edge of the London Eye as it went on its slow rotation.

She smiled widely at him, eyes shining, "Quite the surprise. I had no idea there would be this kind of view from here. I was expecting a rather dingy gallery café."

Joshua was smiling but his tone was serious. "Oh. You underestimate me. I want to always give you surprises. I hope that all our outings together can have this kind of magic. I am delighted you like it here."

At the table, he ordered wine. He seemed to already assume that this would not be the short lunch she had planned for their first meeting. Her presence at the seminar in just over an hour suddenly held very low priority.

He took her hand on the tabletop. His fingertips very slowly caressed in circles around and around her palm. Her hand turned over at his silent command, as if it had a mind of its own. His finger traced the veins and creases on the back of her hand. She turned it back over and he traced her lifeline, long and unbroken. A confident, assertive line that suggested long life and successful outcomes.

His question came to her through a fog, breaking her reverie. "Well?"

"Hmm?"

"I am wondering what the answer is."

She recalled his letter, his fantasy. This was the image he had described, except in his fantasy it had been she who traced her nails across his hand.

Isabella looked up at him through her lashes. "You'll have to wait and see."

Isabella twirled some pasta onto her fork and lifted her gaze.

"Show some patience and reserve," she teased.

Joshua directed an arch look back at her. "Me? Reserve? That's not really in my nature. I'm impulsive, spontaneous… I send passionate letters to beautiful ladies I have only just met." His teasing tone matched hers.

"Oh? Tell me more. Lots of ladies?" Isabella relaxed back in her seat, sipping her wine.

"Actually no, yours was a first. And yes, don't look at me like that, I will explain the woman at the station. I prefer though that we wait just a little longer for all the detail," his voice trailed off as he sensed that Isabella had turned away to gaze out the window, "Oh dear, I see that you want to know, need to know, before we go any further. Right?"

"Right." Isabella returned his gaze this time, green eyes locked on grey.

"Alright, you deserve that, at the very least. Ok. Yes, that woman is, was, my wife. Her name is Frederica, Freddie. I say was, because we are estranged, it's all kind of over. That's why I was so surprised to see her there that day. I have not seen her for weeks. She has been away. But it's also complicated. Difficult. Hard to explain."

"Explain away. I have time." There was an edge now to Isabella's voice, the beginnings of irritation with what was starting to seem like the old cliché, the misunderstood husband, the nagging, distant wife.

Joshua noted her tone, he reached for her hand. "Hey, try and trust me. There's lots to tell. And I will. I want you to understand. But I also don't want us to spoil our first meeting with all of that. Can we agree to park it with more to come later, as we get to know each other? I have a history. I am sure you do too. When we are as old as we are, we both must come with some baggage."

Isabella was conflicted. Would she give this man the benefit of the doubt, agree to allow him to buy some time? Wait to see if there was any possibility of an 'us' before she needed much more from him on the 'them'. It all felt very familiar. And she had been so hurt before. The back and forth of ending marriages, the dance of commitment. Did she have it in her to go through it one more time? The hesitation and doubt were clearly written in her eyes and clenched jaw as Joshua felt her withdrawal.

"Isa...Isa, please look at me. I really want us to find if we have something. To give it a chance. Can you accept for now that Freddie and I are working out some kind of arrangement where we can lead more separate lives. We have children together. But more on that later as well. Can you bear with me?"

Isa touched his hand. Tentatively at first and then held hers palm up for him to grasp. A gesture of conciliation, agreement, but just for now, not complete acquiescence. She was not rolling over. Not again. She would voice her terms when it came to it.

"Alright, for now. But I reserve the right to keep asking. OK?" She noted his vigorous nod and his shining excited eyes. "Let's go back to where we were. I recall you starting to tell me more about you."

CHAPTER FIVE

So that was hurdle number one neatly navigated, Joshua thought to himself, unsure however if it was jumped exactly or just side stepped until more inevitable questions came. Watching her he mused about just how much he wanted this woman, and in particular just how much he wanted her to sit for him. He saw her mouth twitch and heard the lilt to her voice, and he considered the truth of how much she had dominated his thoughts over the past several weeks. Was it all just about his art, and sex? Was he that shallow? Or could she be the something and the someone he had been missing all these years?

"Hey, it's your turn to drift away. What were you thinking?" Isabella was now smiling at him, and her warmth had returned.

"Hmm … I was back in my past, wondering where I would start. I am rather the black sheep of the family. The artistic one. They are all lawyers – my older brother, and our father before he retired." Joshua glanced away his words jogging memories. "Although you might think me to be English in this get up – the eccentric artiste in musty, bohemian attire – I must admit that it's a bit contrived." He broke his gaze from Isabella's eyes again, then looked back, flushing. "Well, not really contrived. I like these kinds of clothes, always have. But I am actually from Australia, brought up in Melbourne, public school and all that – private school they call it there – big house in the leafy suburbs, mother doing Good Works. You know the kind of thing."

Isabella studied him, was he being a little defensive? Adopting this apologetic tone? "No, not my thing" she answered with some heat. "My history's been very different. Quite the opposite. My father died when I was fifteen. I am originally from here but went to the States years ago with the man I later married. As a kid, I had to help my mother run a small hotel in Bath. My sister is four years younger, so she was not much help until later on when I was able to go away to college."

This reminiscing scratched the surface of many mixed feelings. Sadness and regret tinged with some old resentment, plus guilty relief about her hard-earned freedom and independence. She continued more pensive now, the heat had gone. "I suppose I always fantasized about your kind of people, the privileged ones who could lay about and travel and read books whenever they wanted."

Joshua raised an eyebrow, noticing how Isabella set her jaw. "I hear some bitterness there."

"Well, life was very busy for me for years." She shrugged. "I wanted to help my mother, but I missed out on a lot. My friends at college had lots of fun, but

I needed to go home at weekends to help out." The memory of regret clouded her eyes. Shakily she put down her glass.

"So, what did you miss out on?" Joshua sat forward, gently touching her hand.

"All the parties, the boys, the amorous games, the lusty, sweaty looks across the rugby and soccer fields … that kind of stuff."

"What, no amour at all? Nothing during all those years? You are so beautiful … was it all wasted in the little hotel?" He gazed even more intently into her eyes, watching for every nuance.

" Well, no, not completely, I suppose. There were a couple of men, situations ..." Isabella broke off, unsure what she was feeling. There was comfort in his touch, warmth, it was intoxicating. His intensity was compelling her to tell more, to open up. But instead of relaxing her it made her anxious. It was all coming way too fast. She must watch herself, take care.

"Aha, you are intriguing me. And you say men – not boys, this suggests flirtations with older men? Am I right?" Joshua pressed.

"I suppose …" Isa hesitated, her napkin twisting in her fingers, "the boys at school and college always seemed so stupid, immature, gawky. The one chance I had to go to a ball in my second or third year at Bristol, we all went in a group and I ended up with one of the rugby guys – so sloppy, unrefined, inexperienced. Not his fault I suppose, but not at all like I imagined."

Isabella broke off, unsure just how far to go. But Joshua's gaze was still intense, as if genuinely wanting more. He squeezed her hand, encouraging her. So in she plunged saying jerkily, "In my daydreams – I was always a great dreamer; in between hotel chores, I read and dreamed in the garden or in my room – the men were *men*, not boys. Experienced, charming, and expert lovers."

"I see. But hey, don't look away. I get it. I have a lot to live up to if you've been dreaming so long! These older men then, were they just fantasy?"

"No," she stuttered, "they happened." Isabella gently withdrew her hand and picked up her glass.

"So ... lots of stories to come. This is just how I imagined you. Full of wonder. A combination of wistful longing and thwarted experience. There was a mystery to you that drew me to you the first time I saw you with your eyes closed in the train."

Joshua exhaled, inside as well as out. He felt some of his tension melt away as he had watched her listen to him, and now noted that she was more relaxed and willing to share. He had listened intently to Isa's descriptions. Though lots was still missing. He suspected that she had been trampled along the way by men. Men who all wanted to be in her light as well as in her pants. Joshua had been anxious about how he would broach the Freddie issue, and how much to say at first. This opportunity with Isa he did not want to screw up, not before it had even got started. But one step at a time. He knew that he needed to prove she could trust him. And that she needed to feel safe.

So, he had been watching her, just as she imagined. Bella studied his earnest expression. He was such a dreamer! He seemed thirsty for information, almost too eager. But she wasn't comfortable discussing the previous men in her life. Not the real men who'd had an influence on her.

She considered for a moment telling him about the photographer. The one who had come to her mother's hotel and kept returning through the years. Mr. Victor. The first time he had taken her picture, she had been eight.

Why was she thinking of it now? Could it be the way Joshua was looking at her? It was the same way the photographer had looked at her. Hungry. Raw with something like longing. Like he wanted to open her up and scoop out every part of her.

She was tempted. He is very *tempting*. But no, she wasn't ready to speak of such things to Joshua. Not yet.

The period of prickly tension had passed. They seemed to have reached a truce for the moment. Isabella was feeling mellow now, warmed by the wine and the company. Above all, she was liking the attention, but she glanced at her watch. What should she do about the seminar? She had mentioned it in her letter. Did Joshua expect her to skip it?

She felt vaguely resentful about that. Was he already making assumptions about her availability? She had a fleeting image of Simon that last time at the Porters lodge. His intense look searching her face for connection, acknowledgement. What was her own level of availability? She shifted her focus outward again as Joshua's eyes lingered on her lips as she savoured her last bite...

And would she let what he had said about his marriage weigh with her? Of course, she should. But the way he looked at her made her shiver inside, and she wanted him. She wanted to feel his touch. After all the letters, the fantasies, anything else would be a loss. But the internal debate continued. What did she *really* want? She had learned enough about herself to know that trying to settle for something superficial, no strings, never worked. Her history was screaming. Those other men she wasn't ready to tell Joshua about. Their unavailability. Or, worse, their inconsistent availability. She'd never known where she stood or what she could count on. Was it this that was making her paranoid that Joshua would treat her the same way? Would this be just another interlude of episodic intimacy. The other woman, again. The idea rose up like a barrier between them.

Joshua caught the shift in her mood. "What are you thinking?"

"Honestly?"

"Of course. We shall be nothing if we can't say the truth."

Isabella took a breath and looked at Joshua squarely. "I am thinking about several things. How drawn I am to you. How I want to stay here longer. How I feel torn. I really should make an appearance at the seminar. Even if I'm late, I ought to be there for the discussion afterwards. But…what would be your agenda for the rest of the afternoon if you got to choose?"

Joshua didn't answer for a moment, folding his napkin on the table before looking at her. He fidgeted with aligning the napkin edges, then met her eyes. "Yes, it is time for us to be direct. I have made no secret of finding you very attractive. Very desirable. I want you. I want to make love to you, with you. I want to take you to my house. I want you to see my work. I want to paint you. Seeing you again … I want you in my life. I do not want you to disappear again. Is all this so very selfish?"

It was Isabella's turn to pause. "Yes and no. I suppose it depends on what we both want. And if those wants are compatible. It is maybe too early to talk about commitment, but …

"You are very direct."

"It was you who said be honest and direct."

He sat in silence. His head down, his fingers still fidgeting. Isabella was conscious of her disappointment. It crept up through her stomach, disturbing the wonderful food she'd just eaten, turning it sour. What had she hoped for? A more definitive declaration that he was free. He had explained that he and Freddie were 'making arrangements' but doubts crept back in from her past. She recalled all those years of being jerked around. In that moment it did not feel enough.

Joshua knew right then it could be a turning point. He needed to tread very carefully. On the one hand he did not want to mislead Isabella and be later caught in an even deeper deceit. But he also knew he must give her sufficient reassurance that they could move forward, continuing to work out what might be possible. Patience, patience was his mantra for now. "As I said before," Joshua said softly finally raising his eyes to hers, "These things are complicated. Be patient. I believe it will all work out. As they say...if it is meant to be..." his voice gentle but persuasive. "Let us go back to my studio and talk more there."

He leaned towards her to brush a strand of hair away from her eye. His touch was intimate. She liked it, but also resented that he would touch her that way, given the turn the conversation had taken. He hadn't really answered her. And was that an answer in itself? The mood was spoiled for her. Everything was spoiled.

She turned her face away from his touch and lifted her hand for the check. "Not today. I think I need some air. And I need to make this seminar."

The corners of his mouth turned down, making him seem younger suddenly, and Isabella resisted the urge to reach out and smooth away the small frown that had appeared on his brow.

"A moment ago, it was 'should' and 'ought'. Now it is 'need'." Joshua shook his head slightly and seemed to collect himself. "I am disappointed, of course. But I do understand. I know we have something here. It is too good to give up, and too good to damage. So, we shall work something out. What about Kew? It is a little early for some things, but the bulbs should still be good. And if it rains, there is always the palm house to shelter in."

She wanted to cave immediately and bring back the genuine smile to his mouth, the warmth to his eyes, but she resisted. "Another day. I'll write to you. Let you know when I'm in town again."

Her watch told her she would be late. The waiter hadn't yet arrived with the check. A few short moments ago, she wouldn't have cared, but now she wanted to bolt. She had to run. She half stood.

Joshua had caught the waiter's attention. "This is my treat, of course. But I see you must hurry. Yes, but let's not get too serious. It ruins the tone. We must not get too heavy right now and destroy our lovely lunch. After all, it is our first date, one to remember! Off you go. Do you want me to come down with you?"

Isabella did not want to say goodbye downstairs. She shook her head violently, suddenly too choked to speak.

"No, no," she got out. "I'm sorry to have to leave so soon."

He reached out and clasped her hand as she moved away from the table and halted her escape.

"I shall write to you Isa; I shall hold you to your promise."

He watched her go, feeling a sense of deep loss and regret he had not really anticipated. Hmm… he said just under his breath, patience, patience.

Hampstead, London N8
10 April

Bella,

I cannot get you out of my head. I returned from our lunch desolate though the time we spent together was magical. I wanted to swoop you up and throw you over my shoulder and take you off to the country and ravish you. This is what I wanted – did you know? Do I shock you?

Now I have seen you again in person, I shall always call you Bella, like the Italian bella, bellissima, so beautiful, a perfect word just for you. It just rolls off the tongue, so rounded and moist and wonderful. Like luscious wine, or juicy fruits. I imagine the taste of you. But I am running ahead of myself. It is hard not to, for I carry images of you around in my head during the day. At night I am restless, wakeful. Wanting to see you, to touch you. I wonder if you are thinking of me?

I know I did not answer your questions to your satisfaction. Give me that chance. Meet me. Let us talk about everything, know each other better, intimately. Let me explain.

How can I wait to hear from you again? I must see you. Write to me and say you will meet me at Kew.

Your own J.

CHAPTER SIX

Walking through the gardens, they passed through the gate and a pond appeared on the left. Scudding clouds threatened rain, but it was holding off for now. And she did have her Botticelli umbrella. The gardens were almost empty at this still early hour, though a school party approached from the distance. A straggly line of children with coats half off and backpacks bouncing, laughing, and jostling each other on the grass. Still energetic, not bored yet. The day had just begun.

A breeze played at her skirt. When the sun did peep out, it was warm enough to leave her coat open. She had settled on boots and Indian cotton, filmy, soft, a caress against her thighs. She had discarded tights and decided on the cozy sweater that was ribbed in at the waist and accentuated her breasts. She had wrapped and decorated the gift she would offer to him.

Isabella had reflected long and hard about what she was doing. All the way through the seminar, she had replayed lunch. She might as well not have gone to the seminar at all. On the train back, she recalled the way he had clasped her hand before she left. As the days passed, she was quite aware that she was waiting for the letter, had hoped it would come. And when it did, she could not ignore it. She had decided to have this day if nothing else, regardless of what she might find out about him. She no longer felt like running. Almost as soon as she had left the gallery, she had regretted it, had wanted to turn back, and accept the situation for whatever it was, so long as she could experience the sensation that went with it.

She was feeling languid. Now she had decided, just for today, her barriers were down and her sensuous self was emerging. Already her warm secret places were moist, wanton. Did he know? Oh yes, she was sure that from the start this morning, she had transmitted a willingness for what would come today, a readiness. It was just a matter of time. They walked the gardens, letting it build and build. She could let it dangle a little longer, a few more hours. She just loved this tension. This slope of desire. The curving upwards towards the inevitable. It may never be like this again.

Joshua led her towards the palm house. Inside it was warm, dank, with tropical smells and wet air that kissed her cheek. She breathed it in deeply, loving the dampness in her lungs, feeling the moisture seep inside. The foliage was luxuriant. Vibrant, green, waxy leaves, hanging tendrils of vines and aerial roots. A jungle in a cage. There was so much growth she lost sight of the glass enclosure. They were alone in their green and damp corner of the world.

Her light-headedness made her stumble; she was suddenly breathless. Joshua turned and reached out for her. Their kiss was searching. Her lips discovered his softness, his mouth warm and moist. His tongue was already exploring, slithering, sliding, now hard against hers, pressing, pulsing, urgent, then relaxing, as if waiting for her response. The answer came, flicking and dancing in his mouth.

He groaned. "Oh God. Bella … Bella."

His mouth pulled away from hers and he kissed and nuzzled her neck, up behind her ears. She inhaled him, pungent and spicy, but also damp, musty, sensual … male. She breathed in his hair, deep into her nostrils, as he bent lower. His hands held her waist. Moving them inside her coat, he massaged the base of her spine in little circles, gradually widening them so that he was caressing her hips and buttocks in one sweeping movement. The thin material of her skirt would tell him what lay beneath. One hand moved faster, more insistent. Feeling the curve of her bum, exploring the cleavage between her buttocks, finding the crease below and stroking, stroking, stroking. Over and over. The other hand moved to her breast. It crept across the surface of her sweater, exploring the soft mound. He weighed the flesh in his palm, learning its shape and size. Searching out her nipple, he squeezed gently. It was her turn to moan.

"I want you. I have wanted you from the first. I want to be inside you. To slide right in. To crawl all the way up and feel your cunt lips embrace my cock. I know you will be wonderful. You are so lovely."

She felt his erection against her hip. She rubbed him with her pelvic bone.

He drew back. "I want to come with you, together, not before, not here. Shall we leave now or keep teasing each other some more?"

"Let's walk some more," she replied, breathless. "I want to find that special tree. The wondrous one where the flowers come before the leaves. We have all day. I want you to be panting for me. Not actually fucking until we are alone, in comfort, in a lovely, cozy bed."

"God, I don't think I can go on like this all day. Is this a test? You are so tasty, like a very special dessert. Are we leaving the best till last?"

She laughed and straightened her clothes before they walked back outside. "So, if I am a dessert, what am I?"

"Oh, decadent meringue – like we had in Australia when I was a boy. Pavlova it's called. A little crusty on the outside and soft as marshmallow inside, then luscious, whipped cream all over the top and masses of passion fruit dripping down the sides."

"Crusty?"

He took her arm and entwined it with his once more. "Yes, but with you the crust is your strength of character. You are confident and assertive; you know what you want. It is very alluring."

"I'll have to think about what dessert you would be. Crème brulée perhaps … runny and soft with a decadent, burnt-sugar topping. Or flaming crepes with wild strawberries. Though, actually, I don't think of you as dessert. You're more a whole meal. But an exotic meal that goes on and on. Indian, perhaps, or Thai. Certainly Asian. With lots of courses, in small servings, which have surprising spice and heat. A combination of flavours which are unexpected together. Sweet and sour, hot and cold, sugar and spice. Like chili and chocolate … the Mexicans do that. It is quite amazing."

He laughed. "How do you know so much about food?"

"My mother and the hotel. She was always experimenting. She read about food, tried recipes out on us and the guests. She did dinner for everyone in the summer. We would often set up the tables in the garden under the trees. If it was a warm night, it was really beautiful. The flickering candles on the tables. The perfume of roses and peonies. The light made the garden cast lovely, leafy shadows and the gloom covered up how the hotel was really falling apart. So much of it went downhill after Dad died."

As she spoke, the images of the crumbling garden wall and peeling paint under the eaves came back clearly, along with that poignant sadness that was just under the surface, so easily triggered when she thought of her father.

Joshua glanced sideways at her, then kissed her gently. "Let's not go down that road too far right now. It makes you sad. I do want to hear about it, but somewhere where I can comfort you properly. Did you know that when you think hard thoughts you have a little crease just there, and there … and there …"

Isabella let go of the memories and lost herself in the moment.

They followed a path away from the main gate. The rhododendrons were not in bloom, but there were daffodils. Masses of yellow heads glinted in the pale sunshine, brightening the path. The forest of dark green became thicker the deeper they walked towards the woods beyond.

"It will be amazing here in a few weeks," Isabella sighed.

She was trying to focus on everything around her to get away from the intensity of the arousal she had felt in the palm house. She wanted to play it slow, draw it out. The plants made a screen against the world as they walked. She heard a call, a song thrush? Blackbirds were there for sure, and a robin was on the grass grabbing a late breakfast.

Joshua smiled at her. "So, what are we looking for? Where are we going?"

There wasn't a hint of impatience in his tone, and Isabella admired him for that. She was intent on finding her tree.

"There it is!"

Most of the flowers on the magnolia were just beginning to unfurl, although those on the warmer side had opened their delicate skirts to the sun's rays.

"It seems backwards somehow," she said. "The blooms are so large, so summery. To come out like this, before the leaves. To me, it's very erotic, like the tree's abandoned to beauty. The branches are so naked and the flowers so exuberant. I love it."

She turned to look at him, feeling the warmth flood her cheeks.

He was watching her intently. "You are the one who is exuberant! When you talk like this you are quite lit up. I love your expressiveness; that is what I want to capture somehow on canvas. I want to paint you here, where you are so excited about the flowers. It's too early now, but I think in May, on a bench, or standing up with your magnolia behind you. I know this tree too. I've been here before. But from now on it shall be *your* tree. It doesn't matter that the season is a bit wrong, artistic license. I will come back next week to sketch the tree or find one closer to home so that I can get it right. I want to do it when it is in the process of unfurling, disrobing. All those little spring beauties opening their kimonos to reveal their secret charms!"

"You want to paint me in the gardens?" She threw him an arch look. "I thought you would want to paint me naked. Though then it would have to be later than May. A bit nippy! And that would be gossip for the Friends of Kew, or whoever works in the card shop."

Joshua remained serious. "No, not completely naked. Something still vibrant and alluring, but just a little more subtle. But in the gardens, yes. Spring and you in the foliage. Lots of cleavage, diaphanous fabric, backlit with sexy shadows."

Isabella swallowed; mouth dry at the image he conjured.

He stopped and brought her to a halt, holding both her arms. "But to paint you naked – that will remain my privilege at my studio."

Her breath caught in her throat. She no longer wanted to draw out the day, whiling away time in the gardens, beautiful though they were. When she spoke, her voice was husky.

"Take me there now," she said. "Show me."

Waiting to board the train, she felt the thrill of what was to come. To be going home with this mysterious man, in the middle of the day! But then the niggling voice from lunch returned, reminding her of past hurts, of being the other woman. She had lived in triangles before. Is this man really free? Or free enough to meet her needs for emotional security? Joshua had detected her hesitancy. Would he understand if she shared about her past? How would Joshua react?

Should she try and find out before things went any further?

He leaned in and nibbled her ear. "What are you thinking about? You seem very pensive."

She relaxed as his hot breath on the side of her face sent the thoughts spinning away. "I was considering the stories I would tell you, when, how."

"I want them all. Maybe not all at once. I want you to talk to me as I paint you. I plan to do a lot of sketching this afternoon … as well as other things."

"Other things?"

"First I shall titillate you with tasty morsels … wine, hors d'oeuvres, cheese."

"And then?"

"Then, my lovely, I shall seduce you, oh so very slowly. Caress and arouse you until you are dying for me. You'll be begging me to plunge into you."

Isabella lifted her chin. "What arrogance! So you think I can't resist you?"

He remained serious. "No, only I think that you want it as much as I do."

Isabella could feel her body respond again. She was all saliva, mouth-watering, cunt watering, the warm fluidity making her womb feel as if it were melting away. A buzzing started up in her ears.

The train pulled up and Joshua boarded in front of her. He chose a seat at right angles to the window where they could sit together. Isabella moved to one side and sat opposite him instead. She slowly raised the hem of her skirt over her knees, her eyes locked with his. He broke her gaze and glanced down. She made it seem natural, as if she were just adjusting her dress under her coat, all the while drawing the material up higher so he could see beneath it. Her legs were apart enough that he might just make out the beginnings of her clitoris, peeking out between her labia. The surrounding hair would be dark in the shadows, but visible enough to spark his imagination.

A smile danced around her mouth and his lips stretched in response. He cleared his throat. "My dear, you seem to have forgotten something this morning."

Slowly, deliberately, she let her knees fall further apart.

"I've been flashed a few times in my life, but never by someone as beautiful, nor with as much style." His hands had fisted as he spoke. "I want you."

"I know."

The frustrated look he gave her spoke volumes.

CHAPTER SEVEN

Joshua's house was just near the station. It was just as well, as the rain started to come down just as they left the train. They walked quickly, huddling together under her umbrella. The fully expanded Venus was exposed for all to see, and they giggled at the stares directed at them by ladies shopping and a few school kids on the high street. They heard a long low wolf whistle behind them just as they turned the corner. Laughing, they ran through the garden gate and up the steps to Joshua's house, just as the heavens opened and the downpour began.

Joshua fiddled with his keys, his back to Isabella. "Let's go straight in and make a fire. The house will be warm, but I would like …"

She couldn't help it; she stepped back, called by the storm. Not ready to go inside, she stood on the lawn, head cast back, mouth open to catch the raindrops, arms wide to embrace the raw energy crackling around her. She laughed with joy and turned in a circle, eyes closing, feeling the water soak into her clothes, into her skin.

Joshua's arms crept around her waist as he joined her. "I think I just might have to make love to you now. I don't think I can wait."

He licked the raindrops from her neck. She opened her eyes. The door stood open, inviting them in.

She clung to him and kissed him fiercely on the mouth. "Oh yes, but not here … dance with me first and then we'll go in."

He hummed a tango, and they danced on the wet lawn in the early-afternoon April shower. It was cold but Isabella was incapable of feeling any chill. They were exhilarated, together, connected. They were making love before they had even started having sex. The timeless moment ended when Joshua pulled her gently towards the door, still open and letting in the rain. "Come on, inside with you."

He led her through the entrance, along the hall and up the stairs. She could still feel the rain on her cheeks, the music in her ears and the rhythm of the dance through her feet.

She stumbled on the stair, and he caught her around the waist.

She gasped. "There are bubbles rising up inside me, right up into my throat. Like champagne. I can hardly breathe, hardly swallow."

His body pushed hers against the banister. The kiss was long and deep, their mouths hot and wet, their breathing short and shallow.

Joshua broke the kiss. "Let's warm up. Come with me."

The hot water was piercing on her skin. They stood under the water in a shower stall as big as a room in itself. There was room for more than two, with a shower head on each side of the wall. The bench and floor were tiled, lined with shelves full of every kind of shampoo and shower gel one could imagine.

Isabella thought fleetingly that she must have lost time somehow. How had he undressed so quickly? He stood before her, not quite touching, letting the hot water seep into his skin and warm his bones. Then he peeled off her clothes, starting with her sweater. Her arms went up above her head. The wet wool smelled like the gardens in the rain. He dropped it to the floor and discovered her breasts encased in the black bra. He kissed her neck before dropping to visit her cleavage with his tongue. He nibbled the flesh at the top of her bra. Gently, he pulled down the straps and released the clasp. Her breasts fell into his palms. They felt cool. Her nipples were erect from a combination of cold and lust.

Joshua mouthed her nipples, chewing a little and making her moan. "They are so beautiful. I must warm them up."

His hands roamed all over her body, now her breasts, now her neck. He kissed her again, reaching down to peel off her skirt. She gasped for air. She wanted this feeling to go on forever, but she also wanted him to hurry, to just bend her over the bench and plunge right inside her. To fuck her hard and strong. To push into her from behind. She was dying to feel his hardness inside her. All these weeks of waiting. Of imagining this first time. None of her fantasies and daydreams had been as exciting as this, the real thing.

Joshua had grabbed some soapy gel and was lathering her legs and buttocks. She was feeling warm all over and very, very wet. His fingers slid between her buttocks and began stroking, ever so gently, the outer edge of her cunt. Up and down, teasing, exploring. She groaned against his neck. He kissed her deeply, his tongue searching for hers and sucking it hard when her tongue lapped at him. His hand cupped her mons, his finger again searching for her. She stood more firmly with her legs apart to give him more room, stabilizing herself against an increasing likelihood that she was going to faint. He explored inside her, probing her inner secret flesh.

She willed him to move his fingers to the front of her vagina, and as if he read her mind, he delved further. He began slowly using his fingertip to rotate her clitoris as it grew firm and hard under his touch. Around and around, up and down, little fairy touches. Starting softly, he increased the pressure and speed as her breathing increased. She was climbing, her paces mounting, mounting, mounting as she approached the top.

She was flying, lightheaded, about to leap. "I want you inside me. Screw me here, now."

"It would be my greatest pleasure."

She turned her head and glanced mischievously over her shoulder as she bent over the bench.

"Just perfect," Joshua said. He massaged her back, then her bum, as he moved into position behind her. "You don't need to worry about contraception with me," he murmured. "I've been fixed. And I'm clean."

"It doesn't matter about your snip." She held her breath. "I think I am starting menopause."

There, it was out; he could figure out her age now for sure. She trusted him somehow, but why had she told him that? Would it turn him off?

He gently turned her around and held her head in his hands, staring deep into her eyes. "Isabella, I don't care what age you are. You are the most beautiful creature I have ever seen, inside and out."

She turned away from him so he wouldn't see the tears mix with the shower water streaming down her face. Swallowing hard, she reached behind for his cock, which hadn't softened. He stroked and caressed her again and again, kissing and nibbling at her neck and ear lobes. She began rotating her hips in excitement, groaning, feeling exquisite, wanton, free, abandoned. Her buttocks rubbed his cock, teasing him to enter.

She couldn't keep still. "Like this? Now? Now?"

In one sure, smooth movement he positioned the head of his penis just at the mouth of her vagina and he pushed deep inside her. He gasped, then thrust deeper. Isabella moaned, giving low grunts of pleasure. She bent further forward until Joshua was almost kneeling over her on the floor of the shower. The water continued to beat down on their backs and he held her breasts and squeezed then firmly.

Deeper and deeper, the pressure built. Isabella knew she was about to climax, the sensations were growing, escalating. Joshua changed position and gripped her hips.

He was thrusting with purpose now, murmuring, "Are you ready?"

She groaned in assent as he pushed harder. Her uterus was contracting; her legs began to feel weak, her heart beat faster and her mind closed over. His body convulsed above hers as she let go. And then there were waves, over and over, crashing on the shore. The sound of the sea was in her ears. She saw colours – oranges and reds, and as her breathing started to slow, they changed to greens and turquoise.

She came back to herself and stood still, panting.

Joshua exhaled, leaning his weight on her back momentarily before turning her around to face him.

He licked her earlobe and kissed her cheek. "You are magnificent."

CHAPTER EIGHT

Isabella woke up and looked about her. The last rays of the watery afternoon sun were streaking through the hastily drawn drapes of the bedroom, decorated in various shades of white and cream. Off-white, filmy curtains fell from the tall, multi-paned windows, and equally light draperies encompassed the huge four-poster bed.

The walls were painted the colour of Devon clotted cream, the ceiling a touch darker, with white detailing in the heavy cornice and central rosette. A deep, white carpet coated the floor, and extra rugs lay beside the bed. It was a restful room, so full of light.

The white was the perfect backdrop for the abundance of colour relief in the room. Everywhere she looked, there were paintings and prints. On every wall, there was a glow of colour – reds, oranges, yellow greens, in riotous swirling movement, like the poster art of the early impressionists. She looked at the picture closest to the bed. Figures were drinking and dancing in an outdoor bar or café. The sea lay in the distance, and there were palms and other tropical foliage all around. It was abstract, with many lines and blocks of colour, and it evoked a holiday mood, somewhere warm with vibrant light and long, purple shadows.

She glanced at the bedside clock – five o'clock. They had been asleep for an hour or so, exhausted from cavorting in the rain and steamy sex in the shower.

Isabella studied Joshua as he slept beside her. His face had taken on that innocent caste of childhood. His head lay on the white pillow with his hair spread out, damp and tousled from all the activity. She gazed around the room again in the fading light. She could see the streetlights coming on and the rain still coming down outside. She slowly got out of bed and crept across the carpet, not wanting to waken Joshua.

The hallway had several doors opening off it. Trying the first, she was delighted to find what could only be the studio. Even in the half-darkness, she knew it to be amazing. She breathed it in. The scents were numerous and complex. Overall, the heady mixture was foreign, exotic, filled with jasmine and lavender, citrus, and the damper, earthy smells of bark and moss. Mixed with all of these was the expected scent of an artist's workplace – paints and turpentine. Turning on a lamp, she shed light on the high-ceilinged room.

The first impression was of richness and detail. It seemed that drapery was everywhere – the sofas, the curtains, the windows, several alcoves, and cushions of every hue, size, and texture were scattered about, on the floor as well as the furnishings. There were

Persian rugs and camel bags, brass-topped tables and hand-carved stools of many sizes and heights. Brocades, velvets, damask, silks and satins, with tassels and bobbles and swags – it was a decorator's dream! Anywhere else, it would have been overdone, way over the top, but the groupings of colour and fabric created intimate areas in the large space. There were obvious work places and sitting places. Places to be alone and places to entertain. There was even a divan bed in one of the curtained alcoves, covered in more cushions and pillows, and blankets of warm colour and soft, cozy fabrics. All these spaces were arranged around a freestanding fireplace, which stood in the centre like a hub in a wheel. A hand-beaten, copper hood and chimney glinted in the lamplight.

Joshua must live in here. It is *so* him.

Isabella smiled to herself. The studio revealed more about the man than any conversation to date. It was, at the same time, self-indulgent and generous. It was so full of textures and objects; surprises seemed to lurk around every corner. Isabella was so taken up with it all that she neglected, at first glance, to see the racks all along one wall in which painting after painting were stored. When she realised what lay there, she decided not to look until Joshua extended an invitation. His work was his life he had said. He had also revealed that he had not been working lately, so to look would be a violation. To play Goldilocks and explore was one thing, but she drew the line at crossing a boundary as personal as his work.

The bathroom was beckoning loudly; her bladder needed attention. She left the studio and returned to the hall. Off the bathroom was another door that opened into an almost completely dark room. It was another large space, but this one had different smells attached.

She inhaled deeply again. This time it was perfume – floral, a little spicy, but mostly a light, drifty fragrance that greeted her senses – the scent of a woman.

The fluttering in her chest and the change in her breathing was not arousal now but the beginnings of a panic that was familiar and easily recognized. She partially lit the room by way of a lamp near the door. Isabella gasped. It was decorated with a hundred hues of yellow and gold; it was as if she had sunk into a basket of ripe fruit – peaches, apricots, plums, pears – the summer harvest.

Her gaze was drawn immediately to the table beside the bed. The photographs there were all framed in gilt and gold but one stood out among the rest. It was a double frame, with a photo of a man on one side and a couple on the other. The black and white image of the man had long shadows cast against his torso and legs, outlining his nude form in a classic pose. He was seated in a three quarter turn away from the camera and his face was in profile, but she could still recognize him. He had the same line of neck and shoulder, though his body was firmer. A young Joshua. He must have been about eighteen or nineteen. Isabella was struck by his beauty, and the strength as well as the tenderness of the pose. He was at once vulnerable and invincible, sitting there.

The other photograph seemed as if it was taken on the same day. Joshua had a robe wrapped carelessly around his shoulders. He had his arm around a tall, intense-looking woman who was smiling at him, their eyes level. She was large nosed, not attractive in a conventional way but commanding, carrying an air of dominance and confidence. Joshua was looking straight at the camera through a cloud of cigarette smoke. The shot was backlit and there was a halo of light around their heads.

Other photos ranged in age, showing the couple in later years. Her heart sunk further as she discovered those more recent. To keep and display such photographs did not suggest that these were the relics of a past relationship. Besides, the room smelt too fresh; it was lived in. This was no stale marriage or disinterested partner. Her brain began to beat a well-worn tattoo. He had misled her. Freddie seemed to be still very much an 'is' not a 'was'.

She should cut and run.

But now she was in *her* room, curiosity won out. It drove her to open the closet. There were long gowns and coats and shoes. There were racks of blouses and skirts, hung in sets according to colour, texture and season. There were pants and sweaters and belts and scarves, all carefully folded and pressed and very, very organized. Not a sloppy housekeeper.

Definite signs of a compulsive personality, Isabella thought, hot tears stinging her eyes. I wonder how much she needs to be in control. Perhaps Joshua is trapped. He must be trapped. I'm his escape. But just a temporary one. She's away. She's coming back. I shouldn't be here.

Isabella looked further, unable to leave. There was another rack behind the clothes she'd already seen. Her hands paused in their rummaging. *Suits?* Men's suits. Jackets, pants, waistcoats, shirts and ties. There were day suits in different colours and fabrics and several dinner suits, a white jacket, a black tailcoat. Several hats, including a black top hat. Leather boots and men's shoes were all stacked on a top shelf. But they all seemed too small for Joshua. She checked the size of the jackets and shoes and was convinced. And the cut … it suggested they were to be worn by a woman. Perhaps this was all more complicated than she imagined. She should give Joshua the opportunity to explain and show what the situation truly was.

A large painting above the fireplace caught her eye – pomegranates and peonies. The composition was simple but alluring. The style was again strong shapes and slashes of colour, and there was no confusion about its meaning and significance. Wet and luscious. The flesh of the fruit was opened to reveal its private bloody interior and the delicacy of intricate patterning of folds within folds of flower petals.

Erotic … open and abandoned, wanton, screaming lust. Isabella could feel her body respond as she gazed at the work. Her mind kicked in with a million questions. Was it one of Joshua's? Or purchased by … his wife? But it was such an intimate picture. And to have it right there, by the bed, she must know the artist. Or was she an artist as well? There was so much to ask Joshua.

Isabella knew she needed to leave. Joshua might wake up and come looking for her. She stole one last look at the woman in the photographs, imagining her in a suit, with a collar and tie and a long cigarette holder. The image was very powerful. The Marlene Dietrich look. Definitely the woman outside the station standing stiff in the rain. She wandered towards the door, stomach churning. What did this all mean? He must have known she'd find out. Or did he not expect that she'd see more than the hallway and one room? One room and the shower, of course. Would it even matter to him that she was upset?

Her blood was quickening. The urgency was rising to get out, to run out of the room, out of the house, back to Cambridge and as far away from all this as possible. Her pace lengthened as she moved through the other door to the room and back into the hall. She slipped on the rug and almost tripped over a hall chair that was almost invisible through her blurred vision. She groaned as she struck her foot on the corner of the half-opened bedroom door.

"Isabella? Is that you?"

CHAPTER NINE

Isabella sat down on the side of the bed and Joshua reached over to turn on the lamp.

"Hello you," he said gently. He looked deeply into her face. "I can't have you hurting yourself the first time I let you out of my sight. And in my own house too. I'd better be careful, or you won't want to come back!"

He picked up her hand and, turning it over, kissed the palm lightly.

Isabella was in turmoil. Here he was again being so charming and tender. It seemed so genuine. Was he for real? How could she reconcile the actions of this seemingly loving man in front of her with what she was thinking and feeling in the other bedroom just a few moments ago? Her mind raced, thoughts tumbling over each other in their frenzy to get out. She knew enough about herself to know that she needed some space, some time to digest it all. But what were the facts? She needed to know the truth.

"What is it, my angel? You look so pale. Are you feeling alright?"

"Joshua ... we need to talk."

"Of course! What's wrong? What's happened? Oh Bella, you're crying!"

To her dismay, despite all her attempts at control, Isabella found herself unable to stem the tears. A whole history of rejection and pain fed them. "Joshua …" She tried to keep her voice calm, to sob and stutter would just be too humiliating. "I went to the bathroom, and I got the doors mixed up and I went into the other bedroom. I saw there that your … wife … seems very much in evidence. She is still living here, right?"

Joshua was silent a moment. "Well, I did tell you that there was more to explain."

There was just the beginning of an edge to Joshua's voice. A note of defensiveness that put Isabella on her guard. Her tears stopped. He shifted uncomfortably against the pillows.

"Look, Joshua." Her voice was clearer now, stronger. It had a bite. "I know I shouldn't have gone wandering into her room, but I did. You said you were working things out. You led me to believe you were living apart. What I saw there made me question everything." Isabella's voice rose as she started to respond to what Joshua was *not* saying. He wasn't exactly rushing to reassure her that everything was fine – that Freddie was gone, nothing to him now.

"What am I doing here? Has she gone?"

Isabella rose from the bed and strode to the window, swiping open the flimsy drapes to stare blindly at the rain beating on the glass. He had deceived her. He was using her.

"Stop." Joshua's voice was measured. "It is a complicated situation that will take some time to explain. That's why I didn't want to get into all of it then, our first real time together. I had planned for us to discuss it all here, before anything happened, but you were just so irresistible … I couldn't wait to make love to you. I'm so sorry. I don't want to upset you."

He still hadn't told her anything. It was an answer without an answer. But she wanted to hear him out, foolish as it might be.

She turned back to face him. "I had decided to come for today, really no matter what. But I was still thinking, I suppose hoping that ...", she broke off, then continued with a strangled voice, "Just tell me."

He sat up, becoming more business-like, as though he had somehow regained control of the situation. "Right, let's go into the studio, light the fire and get comfortable. I have some special nibbles I planned for us to have, but we …"

He grinned. His eyes lit up. She could see herself reflected in them. They were deep, grey pools. Perhaps he had avoided saying much about his marriage – was still avoiding – not to deceive her, but because it really was complicated. She relaxed her shoulders; everything ached from holding herself so stiffly. He was looking at her questioningly. She took a breath and nodded.

Isabella settled herself onto the sea of cushions that lay before the fire in the studio, not revealing to Joshua that she had already seen it. Joshua lit the fire. The glow, reflected by the copper hood, lit the space immediately around the fire with bright orange light that muted to a warm yellow as it spread further out, revealing the more distant shadowed spaces. The light bounced and danced off the coloured fabrics, twinkling from the silvery and gold threads and mingling with the warm woods and beaten brass. Joshua lit incense and candles. The scent was subtle and the shadows long and mysterious.

It was an exotic fairyland. An Aladdin's cave, evocative of a North African bazaar, minus the crush of the crowds. All the advantages of the sights and smells but better, as it was all private.

Her feelings were still in turmoil, but she couldn't help exclaiming as she looked around. "This room is so extraordinary … quite wonderful. It must be inspirational."

Joshua looked at her with swift appreciation. "Yes, it is a great space. I love it here. But for so long now I haven't felt inspired. My creativity dried up. I hadn't felt the urge to paint anything for ages. And then I saw you in the train. You've changed all that. I must paint you. I hope to do some preliminary drawings soon, perhaps tonight. Look! This is what I used to do ..."

Joshua moved to the side racks and began pulling out paintings and propping them against the furniture.

Had he forgotten why they'd come in here? Her stomach had fallen again when he talked about painting her as though it were a given, she would stay and swallow whatever excuses he made. She tried to collect herself to get him to focus on the conversation they must have. But Joshua's activity distracted her. He placed painting after painting against the walls and on the empty easels dotted around the studio. In just a few minutes, Isabella was surrounded with a riot of colour.

Paintings of so many different sizes, media, and composition. She felt overwhelmed, as if she had been thrown into a churning tank of paint. She felt that she was drowning in colours and shape and form. She stood and, putting her fears to one side, wandered around the room looking closer. Even though the subject matter often differed – landscapes, seascapes, fruit, flowers, groups of people – the approach was consistent. Mad slashes of colour, rainbow hues, jewel tones. The mood was consistently excited, euphoric, even manic.

"Incredible," she said, meaning it. "You certainly were inspired."

"See." Joshua gestured with a wide sweep of his arm. "Given the level of excitation I need to reach before I can pull something like these off, it requires something, or someone, very special, to get me going again."

"So that's now my responsibility?"

"Most definitely," Joshua said seriously, reaching for her as she sank back on the cushions.

They kissed deeply. His tongue found hers and their breath intermingled. Isabella couldn't believe she was letting this happen but felt herself taken over once more by his immeasurable attraction. Passion was just a hair's breadth away, but she began to pull away. As if tuned into the same frequency, Joshua broke the kiss at the same time.

They looked at each other, slightly breathless.

Joshua sighed. "Let me tell you my story."

CHAPTER TEN

"I told you I grew up in Australia," Joshua began. "Well, I escaped to art school in London."

Isabella had withdrawn from him and settled herself on the cushions to listen. She nodded to urge him on.

"I was working as a model at Slade – earning much-needed money – when I met my wife."

She flinched slightly and Joshua continued hurriedly, "Frederica … Freddie … knew some students at the school. She was older than us, but she liked a younger crowd. We went to the same parties, would bump into each other at the same pubs. It just went on from there."

Isabella gazed into the fire. This was the history, but what about now? What made it complicated? She glanced back at her lover. Joshua's face wore a faraway look. She sensed he wouldn't be rushed, but when he remained silent, she prompted, "I saw you together in a photo, in Freddie's room."

He nodded. "Yes, that was taken quite early on. She used to come and watch me pose. She used to say that she liked watching others watch me. It made her feel special somehow because she was going out with me and they were admiring me ... something convoluted like that. She was always pretty convoluted, but I didn't really see it until much later. It was later when things became complicated."

"Oh?"

"Yes, it became about ownership, control, with her … but I'm getting ahead of myself."

Isabella looked into Joshua's face, searching for something. They had been together a long time then, as the photograph had suggested. Did she really want to know the genesis? Would it help her understand? Was he being straight with her?

Joshua ploughed on. "She was rich. Well, she had a rich daddy. What was I to her? A bit of rough perhaps. The bohemian. An anarchist. I was certainly outside her world and I didn't care two hoots then what people thought. She used to say to me that she liked watching me. I used to wear outlandish clothes, from second hand shops, lots of hats and scarves – it was all very sixties. I was manic, entertaining everyone with my Aussie accent. I did Dame Edna impersonations. Oh, and it was the era of Rolf Harris, so we would have wobble boards and play makeshift didgeridoos in the pub and be generally stupid. I made her laugh I suppose."

Joshua paused again. He seemed caught up in the past, as though he were reliving it. Isabella wondered when he had last recounted his history. Was she the first? Or just the latest in a long line to discover the other bedroom and demand an explanation?

"I had other moods," he went on after a moment. "I'd be smoking in a corner just watching everyone through the haze, with nothing to say at all. I suppose now you would say I was in the 'depressive phase' of some kind of bi-polar thing. Anyway, she would come and take over. Get me home or take me to her place, or a friend's. Make sure I had something to eat, sort of look after me. As time went on, we just sort of took up together and played these roles. I was the clown. I made her laugh when I was up and then she looked after me when I was down … she gave me money."

He lapsed back into silence.

"So ... getting married?" Isabella asked in a small voice.

"Well … that sort of just happened. Or, at least, the reason just happened. We ended up in bed together on a fairly regular basis, especially when I was depressed. She would crawl into my bed and stroke my hair. Sex was pretty uneventful, but it gave me some comfort, and probably helped the down feelings for a while. My therapist said that I used sex to anesthetize myself and not face what I was feeling and why. Probably true, but I didn't go back to therapy to work out any of the answers. Too chicken-shit I suppose. Well, the inevitable happened. Freddie got pregnant. I was horrified – it made me feel so old. See? Selfish to the core. My first reaction was about me. Anyway, she blurted it out to the parents one day and before I knew what was happening there was a wedding planned and everything."

Joshua took a breath. Isabella found herself feeling sorry for the boy he had been. Selfish? Well, who wasn't when that young and supposedly free? So, there was a child. That explained a long marriage, she supposed … though, how old was that child now? Was that why the marriage endured?

"I was caught up in a whole lot of stuff in that family," he continued. "Maybe if I had stayed in therapy, I could have broken away from it all. But I didn't. They offered to support me financially, both of us. This house is theirs, now hers, but it was theirs. We raised the child, even had another. We agreed I would be free to pursue my art, and she whatever she was into. Back then it was the financial markets, later it was horses, and later still other pursuits …"

Joshua broke off. He shifted restlessly.

She looked at him enquiringly, but all he said was, "And that's it. In a nutshell."

"Well, that's quite a story," she said. "But what's the situation now?"

He seemed to pick his words carefully, looking deeply into her eyes. "When I say we agreed we would be free to pursue different things … well, that came to mean more than our careers."

Isabella's thoughts flew to the wardrobe. Had Freddie turned out to be a lesbian? She dearly wanted to ask, but she held her tongue, desperate for Joshua to explain things satisfactorily enough for her to accept the situation. For her to believe that it was a different scenario to the one she was all too familiar with.

"I mean," he stumbled, "there is still a link between us. We have children together. We haven't exactly separated so I cannot say I am a completely free agent – I *am* still married. She and the children live here, though they are away often. But as you saw, she has her own room. And we have … an arrangement. There is no confusion when it comes to you. I am not breaking faith with her – it is not like that. And I don't want to hurt you. We are still connected – you see, I can be honest and direct! But it is, like I say, a complicated situation – a *marriage de raison*."

He held out his hand to her, palm upwards, seeking her touch, asking reassurance. "I find you delightful. Sensual and sexy, intelligent, emotional. I am extremely attracted to you, and I want you in my life. I know this is something to figure out. But I hope … I believe we can develop a relationship on its own terms."

Isabella stared at his outreached hand, her brain buzzing. She wasn't sure what rang true and what didn't. It made a certain sense. At least, his explanation made his behaviour make sense. And it did sound complicated. But her mind hurt from trying to untangle it all. She was suddenly more sure what she wanted.

She moved closer to him and entwined her fingers with his in silent acquiescence.

They relaxed together on the cushions, wriggling down amongst the warmth and softness, covering each other with rugs and blankets and making a nest. They kissed. Not long after, both were naked under the blankets and they came together again, gently and tenderly this time, knowing that the lovemaking had begun to take on a different quality. The caresses were sweet, almost innocent, as if they were exploring a new part of each other. Perhaps it was that they were beginning to get to know each other.

St John's College,
April 25th

J,

What can I say about all that passed between us? I am in a turmoil. You first said that you and Freddie were estranged. But then at the house I discover that is hardly an accurate summary of your situation. You took me to dizzying heights. You loved and cherished me. I then felt betrayed. Crushed by the discovery and significance of your wife, your family.

I do want to trust you, to be able to let you in, to know all of me. And hearing your story does help. But your explanation goes only part way. I still have so many questions. I am not sure. I know I am flip flopping, so that is a warning for me. I am still sifting and sorting. Trying to make sense of it all. And where, or if, I can fit in.

I need some time. I am getting more clear on why I feel so torn. And why I feel so vulnerable. The first for sure has to do with the men in my past who have really jerked me around. Yes, triangles then too. Older, married men. I was flattered by their attention, their desire. Their focus was like a golden, bright light. I was told it was love, I wanted to believe it. To believe they would leave their wives. But they never did. It occurred two, no three times. I told you I was married very early on. Well one of these affairs, the most significant one, broke up that marriage. And regardless of all the promises, and all the planning, we did not get together at all in the end.

But the second reason feels much deeper. Something more about the power of the focus, the adoration. I think it comes from much earlier in my life, and maybe the shrinks would say all bound up with the trauma of the death of a doting father. I feel great vulnerability. And I am drawn so powerfully to need to feel safe. There is a story- quite a long one. But it's time I think for you to know a bit more about me.

When you were sketching me, and I was dancing for you, I had a strong memory. All that crazy, manic swirling and whirling – did I really do that? Must have been the wine! I was reminded. It's been a long, long time since I was like that with a man watching.

When I was a little girl, I was known as Bella. Dad started that. It made me think so much of him when you said you wanted to call me that. When I was about eight years old, and my sister, Jane, was four, we were imaginative children, whiling away the hours in the attics of the hotel in Bath that was owned by our parents. That was a happy time, long before the sadness of our father dying, seven years later. Most days we would play dressing up and let's pretend, working our way through the big trunks of dresses and hats and scarves, a whole assortment of clothing and props which had been handed down by my favourite uncle and aunt, from when they were in amateur theatre.

On sunny days, mum would suggest that we take our games outside into the garden. So, this would mean dragging all the outfits down the stairs. Often, I would change my mind about the details of my outfit, so I preferred to bring lots of options with me. I would change outside under the trees. I didn't care about who might be watching.

The summer I was eight, Mr. Victor came to stay again at the hotel. He was a frequent guest, a single man who seemed very old to me. He would go out each morning walking in the town and return in the afternoon and have tea in the garden. By this time, I would usually be at the hat and gloves stage and serving tea to my sister and our dolls or be dressed up as a teacher and scolding all the pupils for talking in class or acting the doctor and taking temperatures and listening for heartbeats.

On this particular summer day, I was changing hats. I remember I could not make up my mind which hat was the best one. I noticed Mr. Victor watching me from his chair under the trees. He had a camera with him. He had told me before that he always enjoyed my antics in the afternoons when he returned from his walk. He said my games were something he looked forward to all day. I was probably flattered by his attention. I asked him which hat he preferred. He said that he liked them all, and he asked if he could take some photographs. Mother agreed and so I made a big display for the camera, changing hats and striking different poses. The sun went behind the clouds, and it started to rain. We all moved inside, and Mr. Victor asked if he could finish the film so that he could get it developed the next day. I suggested we go to the attic. I was bored with hats and more costumes were upstairs.

Somehow Jane had drifted off somewhere else, so Mr. Victor and I were alone in the attic. I don't recall feeling shy or embarrassed. I just went ahead like I always did, changing costumes, and Mr. Victor took photographs. It did not take very long. I was partly shielded by an old screen when I changed and Mr. Victor watched, but only took photos when I had changed. So it all seemed perfectly fine to me. Then.

Seven years later, the summer after father died, Mr. Victor was staying again. He had come most summers but there had been a gap and I had not seen him for three years. By this time, I had evolved from the ugly duckling stage, and I was becoming well aware of my impact on men when they came to the hotel. They would look at me, watch me in the dining room, sometimes move their shoulder or arm against my hip when I served their dinner. I started to wear big sloppy sweaters or T-shirts to cover up my body.

I was very sad that summer. My father had been my great hero and friend. I missed him terribly and I spent a lot of time in my room alone, reading and writing, rather than going out, or spending time with my friends from school. Mr. Victor seemed to be rather preoccupied with me. I would see him everywhere I went in the hotel, or the garden, sometimes even in town at the shops. I felt him watching me. I didn't really mind. I maybe liked his admiring looks. The attention felt good. But it was a bit creepy how he seemed to be waiting for a glimpse of me behind every corner in the hotel.

One morning, he reminded me of the photo shoot when I was eight. He asked if I still had the dressing up boxes. He was being so kind and gentle, asking about how I was feeling and acknowledging how sad I must be. He seemed lonely too, so I probably felt sorry for him. I decided to show him the attic again. As I stood behind the screen looking at the costumes, I heard him gently ask if I would dress up for him. I remember feeling lonely and empty. I wanted to feel pretty and happy. I was attracted somehow to this man who made me feel special, because he liked what he saw.

The old, much used angel wings had not been worn in years. I took off the baggy T-shirt I wore for hotel chores and put the wings on over the brief white tank top that served as my underwear. Mr. Victor had a camera with him again. He asked if he could photograph me as an angel. This time it was a video camera. I thought that would be OK. In fact, I felt a little thrill of excitement that someone wanted to make a movie of me, however unsophisticated it was. I felt my mood lift. I took off my jeans so that I could move easily and tuned the radio to some music.

I danced and danced. I remember that I twirled and swayed and jumped and fell down. I kicked my legs and waved my arms up and down as I moved around the room. An angel flying from cloud to cloud in heaven.

Mr. Victor was transfixed. Adoring. He gazed at me as if I really were an angel. He moved towards me to get a close up of my face. He moved my hair to expose my neck and asked me to adjust my top so that he could see my shoulders. I pulled down the straps of my tank top. I could feel his breath on my neck as he helped me tuck the straps in behind the elastic of the wings. I recall looking into his eyes. His brown eyes were dark, dark pools and I could see my own face reflected in them. He did not touch me. He did not really do anything much except look. But that gaze! He looked at my bare shoulders and then his look travelled all over my neck, my budding breasts, my face, hair, and lips and he stopped at my eyes. I could feel his longing.

He was able to take a still shot with his video. I kept that photo. He mailed it to me afterwards. He never returned to the hotel. But the photo will always remind me of that day. When I look at it, I see a young girl on the brink of womanhood, with her hair wild and unruly, pulled back behind her ear. The photo is cropped just above her breasts, and you can see her naked shoulders and neck. Peeking up behind her head are the tips of a pair of very bedraggled angel wings. She looks magnificent. Alluring and vulnerable, but also powerful, omnipotent. She has that look that says, "I can do anything!"

Writing all this down now brings it all back. As you would say – it's all very complicated! So you see, lots of reasons why I am hesitant, and questioning. I am very drawn, but I am very scared.

Bella

Hampstead, London N8
10 May

My angel,

Me dearest girl. I don't want you to be scared of me. We must talk more, see each other more. Your letter haunts me. Thank you for sharing some secrets. That man – do you see him as artist or predator? Do you wonder the same about me?
I understand that this man, and those others who were married, have had a big effect on you. You are beautiful. You have had an adoring audience. I know that sometimes this has a big downside. I also have had adoring fans. There can be a cost. I can relate.

It is a nearly a month since we were together! The time has ground slowly by in some ways as I miss you deeply and would adore to see your beautiful smile. But in another way time is flying! And how you flew in that dance! Such sexy memories of our time, but that was such a highlight! It, you, inspired me! I am painting again! As my muse you are magnificent! The painting is coming along. It will be BIG in more ways than one (I'll not tell you yet what that means).
When I close my eyes I see you outside on the lawn, twirling around and around. I was transfixed by your beauty. I could see every wondrous curve of your form. Your hair fell from your neck like a dark, waved curtain. Your face glistened in the rain. You were a

goddess. Of the earth, of the seasons. You performed an ancient rite of blessing and thanksgiving. I was moved. It was right then that I felt compelled ... I was victim of an urge ... an instinct ... to pursue, to take, to possess, to penetrate ...
Your inspiration rises above my anxieties about the mundane and I press on, often all through the night!

I'm up to Cambridge next week to finalize the hanging of the exhibition. It's not until June (to catch the tourists) but the Fitz is getting in a tizz!
Coffee/lunch? Thurs/Friday? I'll confirm in another note when I know.
I am missing you, thinking of you. Though painting you each day, it's as if you are here. I am creating my own YOU to keep with me always. Jx

CHAPTER ELEVEN

Isabella paused outside the porter's lodge; Joshua's note clasped in her hand. She stared across first court, not really seeing the fine lines of the chapel rising into the sky, nor the gaggle of students bottle necking before the entranceway to Hall.

It seemed so long ago she and Joshua had been together. She had thought about him, about them, every day since. The familiar breathiness and tightness in her throat that arose every time she did so always seemed to end with dampness between her legs.

Telling Joshua some of her early life stories drew them that much closer. There was more to tell but she wasn't one to reveal everything at once – a lot like him, she imagined.

In fact, his response to her letter suggested an empathy that she had not credited him with. Being the victims of other people's fantasies could give them something unexpected in common.

She'd been prey to a floaty, dreamy feeling for days. It had started during her dance and persisted. The idea of seeing him again sent shivers through her. She would wait until next week, though coffee or lunch sounded tame compared with the intensity of emotion they'd experienced together in his studio. Did he expect her to invite him back to her room?

When would she be able to see the painting? What she had seen of his initial sketches made it difficult to imagine what the end product would be. She could recognize the shape of her bottom and hips and breasts, but there were so many heavy, black lines, drawn and redrawn, then rubbed out. It was like many different sketches layered on top of one another, so that legs and arms and heads were intermingled together. A swirling mess!

Isabella desperately needed to focus on her university work – she had seminars, and that paper on Cleopatra to finish. There was lots to keep her busy before Joshua came again, but she needed to concentrate. Meeting him – and everything since – had been beyond distracting. Her mood shifted slightly at the thought. She mustn't jeopardize her career, not over a man who wasn't really even hers. Complicated, complicated … how often had he called it that? But would it always be so, or was there a likelihood of a simpler time between them? What would this Freddie think when she saw Joshua was painting again?

Wishing to escape the turn her thoughts had taken, she began walking towards the main gate and the street beyond, when a voice called her name.

"Isa! Isabella! Wait a minute, there's a letter for you."

It was Simon, and he was holding out an envelope. "Here, the mail clerk asked me to give it to you. This was in the last post. Hey what's up? I haven't seen you for ages. We only meet up at the mail pigeonholes! We must go for a drink and catch up."

Isabella reached for the envelope, smiling as she saw her address written in Joshua's now familiar script. It must be his confirmation of the day for lunch already. She itched to open it at once, but she bundled it with his other missive and turned her smile on Simon.

"Simon, thank you! It means I won't have to come out here tomorrow. I've been in London a lot with the Cleo stuff. The sources I am using are at the BM, so I need to be there quite a bit. Lots of seminars at the University of London too. Been busy! A drink would be great. Tonight?"

They walked out into Kings Parade together, jostled by the pedestrians and dodging the cyclists. Isabella was always comfortable in his presence. It was a new friendship, but each time they met up they enjoyed easy talk and warm laughter. Isabella had to admit that she'd been attracted to Simon when she first noticed him in the pub at the beginning of the year. He had a quick grin and blue, blue eyes. They'd met at the bar. She was ordering the next round for her table, and she'd wondered if it were chance that he came up to order at the same time or if it had been by design. He was the Acting Bursar now, while the Bursar was on leave, but it had been a surprise to her then that he was so interested in her work about an ancient past. So much for stereotypes! She had assumed he would be more interested in the money markets and current affairs, but he always seemed fascinated with her talk of the mystery and intrigue of the ancient Egyptian court.

He once even called it a soap opera! And she supposed it was turning out that way, what with the revelations about incest and previously unknown claims to the throne that she and her London colleagues were discovering in their translation of some rare texts.

They walked and talked, dallying on the corner when they came to where they would part ways. As usual, Simon was fun and refreshing. He was so very different to Joshua. The intensity of the feelings generated in Joshua's presence was a stark contrast to this easy, relaxed friendship. With Simon there was none of the agitation or anguish. She never did take the easy road.

They parted having made plans for the evening, and Isabella wondered if she should tell him about Joshua, and if she did, what would she say.

Hampstead N8
10 May (later)

Dearest B.

In haste. So sorry. Next week is off. The meeting at the Fitz will have to be postponed and although I would love to see you anyway, I have to go away. Freddie called and both children are ill and I can't return yet. She has some business meetings she needs to attend to and we don't want to leave the children with the grandparents too long (being a burden and all that). So I've agreed to go back with her to help out and then bring them back here. So will be a couple of weeks I should think before it all gets sorted out.

Sorry, sorry. I am missing you and even worse, I shall miss the painting. It has taken me over!

I'll write soon.
J.

CHAPTER TWELVE

Joshua put down his pen and looked over his shoulder. Freddie watched him through a cloud of cigarette smoke.

"Are you satisfied?" The edge of sarcasm to Joshua's tone didn't mask some petulance. "Will you get off my back now? I'm not going up to Cambridge next week and I'll give you more help with the kids. If you'd told me earlier ..."

Freddie barked a laugh. "Oh, don't give me that. I've been phoning and leaving messages. You haven't returned any of my calls. So, I come down last night and what do I find? You flaked out. Surrounded with wine bottles. The whole place in chaos."

Joshua sniffed defensively but said nothing.

Freddie laughed again, scorn in every decibel. "It's just so obvious. Don't give me that old bullshit. *She's just a model. It doesn't mean anything.*" She was shouting now. "The painting wouldn't be any good if she didn't mean something to you!"

He grinned sheepishly, his sullen look disappearing at mention of the painting. "Magnificent, isn't it? At least we still agree on what makes good art!"

Freddie began to pace up and down the studio, trying to sort out her thoughts and feelings. He had surprised her, and she did not like surprises. Not when it meant that something was going on that she didn't know anything about. Not when it was obviously so significant for Joshua. It had been a long time since anyone, other than herself, had been significant for Joshua. Those affairs in the early years had stopped once they had made their deal. And now? He was painting again. He hadn't done anything great for years. She glanced again at the huge canvas propped on the easel by the fireplace. The colours and form were absolutely stunning. But that was not all. His mastery of movement was amazing. The action was everywhere in the composition – swirling, twirling figures – all the same model but in many, many different poses, some separate, many overlapping, but all integrating into a synthesis of erotic, frenzied dance.

And the movement wasn't even the key achievement. That face, those eyes, that hair – they were by far the most overwhelming elements of the work. It was that woman. The one at Cambridge station with the umbrella. She had realized as soon as she saw it. Despite only having glimpsed her in the distance, she had noted Joshua drop her arm, and the shape of her body had been easy to appreciate, especially from beneath the belted raincoat.

Finding Joshua slumped in the studio in a stupor amidst the carnage he'd created hadn't even given her pause. It was the painting that had sent hot rage coursing through her veins. Vicious, intense, bitter jealousy.

"So, tell me about her Joshua. You lied! You said you did not even know her name! What is she like, your new muse? What did you do together? What makes her so inspirational?"

"All you have to do is look at the painting to see why she is special," Joshua replied, his voice tired now, worn down from arguing, defending his position. "No, I won't tell you all about her, about us. It will take the magic away. And it is the magic that drives the creativity. The drug I need to make it all work. You can't have that. I've given up so much of everything else for you and this family. Not that too."

"*You've* given up so much!" Freddie banged her fist on the table beside him, her face twisted into an ugly grimace, "Look around you – without me you wouldn't have any of this! I don't believe what I'm hearing! You ungrateful bastard!"

"No, Freddie, I *was* grateful. But that was a long time ago. You need control and stability to impress daddy and I need financial support and solitude to be creative. It's quid pro quo."

Joshua had rather surprised himself being so forceful with her. He felt a gleeful grin begin deep in his gut. But not one he could show. She had had so much of the control for as long as he could remember. It was his turn to take some back. But right now, there was so much at stake. He was finally painting and that could not be risked. He better tread a bit more carefully with this.

He slumped further down into his chair, closing his eyes against the trembling shrew standing over him. "What are you really worried about? That if I'm finally successful I might not need your money?"

Freddie stood speechless. A part of her brain not taken up in the rage and resentment marvelled at the change in Joshua. He had never been so self-assured and calm in the face of one of her rages. She stepped away, tossing her head, and catching sight of her flushed face in a mirror hanging from the wall. She forced her breathing to calm before she spoke again.

Okay then, don't ruin your *magic*." Her sarcastic tone was caustic. She moved closer. "But don't forget that we have an arrangement. You cut me off; I cut you off." She came closer still, placing her hands on his shoulders, her breath tickling the skin just below his ear. "Remember Ingrid?" Freddie leaned further forward. She raised her hand and squeezed his ear-lobe hard between her bright red fingernails. "Don't tell me you've forgotten all the fun we've had together. There's a reason you usually keep me in the loop. Wasn't it my idea to introduce Ingrid to her special toys? Her pain was your inspiration."

"That was different," stuttered Joshua.

Freddie practically felt him relinquish control into her hands.

"Yes, I know," she soothed. "But I would very much like to see you inspired again. It's been such a long time. It was such a turn on."

Freddie saw Joshua swallow hard and look away, his body tensing as he moved out of range. So, he'd just needed reminding.

She'd been his muse once. It hadn't taken long to realize she could only ever be one of many. But she was the one who took care of him, and the one who got to keep him. And she'd learnt to accept that she would have to share and had twisted it to fulfil her own desires as well as his own. He belonged to her, and so did anyone he touched. He knew that. He just needed reminding.

"Remember when you used to let me watch behind the curtain? All those young, nubile art students. I would just lie on the divan and watch and …"

"I knew what you were up to. You had your own toys, didn't you? You used to have a great party with yourself. Is that what you want? I thought you had that one-way mirror installed in your bedroom, so you didn't need to bother with my models. I thought they bored you in the end, not enough excitement for you."

"*They* weren't," she said.

No, they didn't compare with what he'd found for himself now, what he'd tried to keep from her.

"Why don't you fuck her in my room? She doesn't even have to know. Just our little secret."

Winnifred stroked his neck and smiled as sweetly as she could, the blood still simmering under her skin.

"I don't know …" he said, but she could tell he was thinking about it, excited at the thought.

He would share. He would want to show her off. Freddie's arousal would validate his own; it had always been that way. He'd probably already thought about her coming across the painting, had been willing her to come home.

"I want to pose her again," he burst out. "Watching that might be okay. But I need time to sort out how it might work. I have a fantasy about the next time."

"Oh really?"

Freddie was intrigued. She was getting excited about the possibility of seeing this woman. Her thoughts were already moving ahead. Would the face, the hair, the eyes, the body match the beauty that Joshua had portrayed? Joshua's smile was sly, vaguely seductive. She decided it would be prudent not to push the matter further. She'd stopped him from going to Cambridge. The next time the woman entered their house would be at her instigation. She'd won.

With a final stroke of his cheek, she left the studio and made her way to her own room. She went straight to the safe hidden behind the suits, at the very back of the wardrobe, the façade of which was the two-way mirror Joshua had alluded to. From the safe, she brought out an album of old photographs from the collection of leather-bound tomes. She caught her breath as she turned the first page, not even bothering to come out of the closet.

Body after beautiful, young body entwined with Joshua. His panting and sweating face, his gleaming eyes, home to that faraway look he would get when he was transported emotionally. Painting was the strongest driver for this, but sex was a good second best.

For him, it was painting; for her, it was photography. She had often zoomed right in on his face as he was about to come. Another shot with a wider angle showed a brunette sucking him off. A youngster with café au lait skin was sucking the brunette's nipples from underneath while he fingered her cunt. She remembered he had just had his turn. He'd been fucked hard and long by Joshua's beautiful, hot cock. The boy was in dreamland, satiated, having expelled his own seed all over the bedclothes. She hadn't entered that scene herself, though she sometimes did. She'd observed them from every position the room had to offer, camera in hand, and only given into her own lust much later, in her dark room, when the prints were in her hand.

Ah, those were the glory days when they were young and foolish! But now, what about the present, and the possibilities of the near future? It could be that way again. Envisioning the woman in the new painting, Freddie did not feel ready to call it a night. Not just yet.

She made herself comfortable in her favourite bedroom chair, feet up, lit toke at hand. Inhaling deeply, the album balanced on her lap she took her time. Marvelling at those forms.

Half closing her eyes she began to drift, relaxed by the pot smoke. Her eyes started to cloud over; the room went out of focus. She just let go to revel in the feelings. Freddie allowed herself to float. Her mind danced towards the images beginning to form. In and around, back and forth, feeling all the languorous sensations. She saw Isabella's face in her mind's eye. She was below her, head cushioned on a damask pillow. Her burnished hair flowing out and down across her shoulders. Her kissing travelled softly, gently like butterfly kisses down Isabella's neck and across her chest, taking nips and nibbles at her nipples, but saving the extended savouring of them for another time. Her mind rushed ahead, fired along by her growing arousal. Freddie touched her cunt. She felt the slipperiness of her own lust. Succulence. She wanted this woman. It was building already. She would take her somehow. Her mind went straight to her target, parting Isabella's knees as she stroked the soft, soft flesh at the top of her own inner thighs. Her focus kept swinging back and forth from the imagined picture in her head to her own pubis and the attention it was demanding.

Her guttural mutterings came from deep in her throat, "I want to study you, to understand the beauty of how you are made, to open you up like opening the petals of a flower or separating the segments of an exotic fruit. I want to kiss and lick and suck every segment of you. I want to explore with my tongue along the creases and valleys of your cunt. And to find that special little nub, under its little hood and stroke and kiss and lick until I drive you wild."

Her fingers stroked and tickled and explored herself as she spoke to her imaginary lover. She knew how quickly she could bring herself off. So practiced. She knew the short cuts. But not tonight. More savouring. Spread it out. Make it last. She pictured the cunt lips and the red, wet opening she sought. The clit, just hiding there, starting to swell, harden. Her own juices mixed in some surreal way to become Isa's and Isa was on top doing this to her, then her mind switched, and she was back doing the lapping. Back and forth, in and out, this was the kind of lap dance she craved! She finger fucked her cunt at the same time as her lover's, and Freddie felt herself rise on the increasing tide of her orgasm. Her thighs clenched, and tweaking and rubbing her clit she tried to stay focused on Isabella, but her own body grabbed her away. Freddie gasped. She heard the deep groan from her own depths just as her mind heard the same from Isabella.

CHAPTER THIRTEEN

Isabella read Joshua's second note of the day back in her room after a long overdue visit to the university library. She sank heavily into her seat at her desk by the window, the disappointment a leaden weight in her gut. It dragged down and through her, leaving in its wake a dark emptiness.

He so casually alluded to his wife and children. To *Freddie*. But the way he spoke to her didn't sound right. Why write in such haste? So briefly? Why not take the time to make further plans, to quell the fears he surely knew she would feel? And his last word had been on the painting. She'd posed for him now; that was all he'd needed her for. Tears welled under her eyelids, hot and stinging, but she refused to let them fall.

Was she overreacting? Perhaps she was being paranoid. Insecure. Shouldn't she rather be feeling a bit of compassion for his children? Complications were part of real life. She surely hadn't really thought they could carry on their affair, and it never be affected by him having a whole life and wife and family, separate to her. Stupid.

But this didn't feel normal. This didn't feel like *life getting in the way.* And she would know, right? She'd been the other woman before. No, all was not well in Wonderland. She dashed a hand across her eyes. He didn't deserve her tears. He was a bastard after all.

Thank goodness she'd made plans with Simon. He would be a good distraction.

Isabella quickly ran a brush through her hair and spoke aloud to her reflection.

"So… is this a use? This drink with Simon? I quite like him but…" Not wishing to stay still long enough to consider the guilt that was beginning to seep into her awareness, she grabbed her jacket and bag, and ran down the stairs. As she entered the corridor near Simon's office several graduate students were milling around, smoking and talking after dinner in Hall. She hadn't eaten all day. All the more reason to go off to the pub for a pint and some stodge. Good comfort food.

'Feed the belly and calm the mind' had been one of her mother's sayings. She could practically smell the bread baking in the hotel kitchen, where her mother would stand stirring soup. She had found solace at the stove, for months it seemed, after her father's death. Her mother had retreated from the world. Isabella had rarely seen her actually eat any of the food she prepared. But she had pushed it on Isabella and Jane and the hotel guests, who loyally kept coming.

Simon was coming out of his office and heading towards the noisy group of students when he saw her.

"Hi there. Don't hang around these fellows – they will poison you with their second hand smoke and corrupt you with their politics!"

The group laughed, breaking off their intense conversation to get out of their way.

Isabella stepped back to let them pass. "How about that drink? How about we …"

She broke off, seeing Simon's smile light up his eyes. He seemed so genuinely pleased to see her. This gave some comfort to the grey corners of her soul. A little of the misery lifted.

He was so much less complicated! He seemed so straightforward. The thought of honest, even simple, conversation with Simon had real appeal.

"Yes, let's go to the Granta," he said. "We can have a bit of a walk and it's not as noisy there."

She linked arms with him without thinking, and they walked together in companionable silence, out of John's and along the Backs in the moonlight. They picked up their friendship easily, just as they picked up their earlier conversation. They talked of work – a fundraiser Simon was heading up and readings Isabella had been doing. She brought Simon up to date on the latest in the Cleo saga and Simon spoke of the cross-Atlantic project he was involved with, which would likely take him across the pond for several months.

Isabella realized suddenly that she'd miss him when he was gone. "So … Harvard, huh? The Business

School? That'll set you up with some good contacts for the future."

"Yeah," he shrugged. "It's all about networking. I'll probably get an offer of a post there if this joint project comes together. Then I don't know. My mother is American. Did I tell you that? She's very pleased that I might spend time over there. There are lots of relatives around New York and the eastern seaboard. So, I won't want for Sunday lunches!"

Isabella smiled at his easy sense of humour. Her own troubles felt far away for the moment.

"Just like you to get it wrong," she teased. "You'll starve. They don't do hot Sunday lunches there. You'd only get a sandwich for lunch. It's all about dinner. Cultural differences you know. Subtle but big!"

Simon laughed and gave her arm a squeeze. She was conscious of a mad moment where she wished she'd never met Joshua on the train. She wished she hadn't been so elusive, just seeing Simon by chance every so often, head down with work and then disappearing to London. She should have made an effort before. Now everything was so tangled up.

"Well," he announced when they were settled with their drinks. "What else is new? I haven't really seen you since March, I guess. There was that time, though, outside the mailroom, when you had that letter. Was everything alright with that?"

Isabella shifted uncomfortably. She should tell him about Joshua. They were sitting cozily together, and he was so obviously interested, and she didn't want to lie about the letter.

"Hey, you don't have to tell me. I was a bit worried that maybe something was wrong, like someone was ill or something. You know. It looked really serious. And I remembered that your mother was on her own and …"

He broke off. He sounded like an awkward schoolboy. Guilt stirred again in her stomach.

Such a nice man. He'd been worried about her.

"Oh, Simon, you're sweet. No, everything's fine with Mum. I'm amazed that you remembered."

She was unsure how she should play this out. He had taken her somewhat by surprise being that direct – well, in an oblique, but not so oblique way. He was clearly asking her what was going on. Did he suspect someone else? And what if he did? There was no real relationship between them. No understanding at all. Just friends. But what was she doing now? Was she taking advantage?

"Oh quit! she told herself impatiently. *Cut the mental gymnastics. Can't I just have an evening out without making it into a complex ethical dilemma?"*

She looked down and toyed with her glass, taking a sip to save from having to say anything for a second.

Simon was looking at her, clearly waiting for a more substantial explanation.

"Well," she said lightly, "a lot has been happening. And yes, some of it has to do with that note. No one is ill or anything – it's not like that. It's more about someone I met … he's in London … so he's been a bit of a distraction …" She faltered. His face had stayed carefully composed, but his grip had tightened on his pint glass for a second, she was sure of it. She rushed on. "But, right now, I'm not at all sure that it's going anywhere. If it's all right with you, I don't really want to go into it. I just want some nice company over a nice drink. I feel like I want to get into a little safe, and protected bubble at the moment, away from all the crap of the world."

Simon cleared his throat and gave her a smile, which seemed forced, but his tone was as light and pleasant as ever when he spoke. "I see a bubble is needed. Well, you've come to the right place. Being an expert in a wide range of business matters, bubbles just happen to be one of my specialties!"

They weathered the awkward moment and, thanks mostly to Simon, the evening progressed very pleasantly. Isabella relaxed inwardly. There was a return to the easy banter and friendly debate of former times together. They covered off movies they had read about but had not had time to see, foods they missed on restricted income budgets, foreign places they dreamed of seeing, politics, family – the usual range of topics friends converse about.

There was a new tension between them, but it was buried far beneath the surface chatter and didn't spoil her enjoyment of the evening. *He almost serves* too *well as a distraction*, she thought.

Outside her college room door, they hugged. He held her just a second longer than friendship protocol would suggest appropriate, but not long enough to take them over the brink. They parted easily, without the need for reassurances about future meetings.

Nevertheless, she fell into bed with a sigh of relief at having come clean, feeling like she'd weathered a storm. She ignored the letter she'd left lying on her desk. What would Joshua have thought if he'd seen them out together? She wished he had.

20th May

Joshua,

Finally, finally I am writing this. I tried to avoid the mess I felt. I had to focus on some work. Have some distractions. But now as I think of you, I still just swing from fury to tears.
I thought we had a special something. I thought you were feeling it too. You said as much. So, what was that...passion in the moment or just outright lies?
Silly me I was waiting for another note. For you to explain more. You were so rude. So abrupt. There was such a disconnect between your two letters. I simply don't understand.
You can't just disappear and then expect me to be at your beck and call and dance to your tune. It's the blowing hot and cold that I can't cope with. It's too much like shit from my past. I had promised myself that I would not get tangled up in this kind of thing ever again.
I have started this letter many times. I feel so torn. Torn between being drawn back in but then repelled away by the pain. And torn up inside. By you.

So now it's nearly the end of another month. Nothing else from you. No card, no flowers, no further plans, nothing. I don't think I can do this again. I just can't open myself up to love and then discover another bastard. Just using me. The swings are too extreme. Sure, love the highs, being caught up in your web, but the cost is too great.

You have to treat me better than this- otherwise I'm done. I may be already.
B.

CHAPTER FOURTEEN

The tube to Hampstead was an easy matter. But then there was the walk. Every step of the way, Isabella considered stopping off at one of the many bookshops to browse, or at one of the cafes to have a latte or tea. Perhaps she didn't need to do this today.

"No," she muttered under her breath. "Time enough for coffee on the return journey."

She walked quickly up the hill, driven by the urgent need to accomplish her task. It felt right, something she must do. She was fighting for her life – her emotional life. Much better than folding. She didn't notice the physical exertion. She wasn't short of breath. Her feet just seemed to fly, skimming over the pavement as she mounted the last of the steep climb to the top. Turning the corner, she forced the image of the rain and sound of the wolf whistle out of her head. She had a job to do.

The letter was in her pocket. She had composed it on the train. This letter was one she needed to deliver personally, but not to save on the postage. It was to give him some unrest. When he got home, he would know, holding the envelope without a stamp, that she had been all the way to his house. He didn't have control over everything, certainly not her.

Let him suffer too, she thought. *I'm a free agent. I refuse to wait around to hear from him.*

Isabella stood for a moment opposite the house. She was about to cross and put the letter in the mail slot when a glance at the upstairs windows stopped her in her tracks. She turned her gaze to the downstairs windows in turn. She had expected them all to be covered with drapes, the house standing in darkness. Joshua and Freddie were supposed to be away in the country taking care of the children at her parents. That's what he had said.

Her heart started to thump and a ringing in her ears became louder and louder as she stood there, rooted to the spot. Every light in the house was on. There were people's shadows, many people, moving about inside. Looking around, more cars than would be normal lined the street and, if she listened carefully, she could catch the strains of music, even from this distance. They were at home. And they were entertaining.

The letter was forgotten. She tore herself away and ran back down the street, her breath hitching. Then the tears came. Hot, angry tears.

As she ran, a voice in her head recited a catalogue of all the other men who had let her down, bailed out, not come through. What had she expected? That he would be different? That bastard. That asshole, pretending he was so sensitive, so sweet, so bowled over by her. Fucking liar!

A woman was standing on the street with her little girl. As she thrust past, the woman's head whipped round, and Isabella realized she was swearing aloud. Sobbing, she made it to the park and collapsed on a bench. She didn't care who saw, who heard. She just cried.

She returned to the station at a slow pace, her head a little clearer. Why didn't he tell her the truth? What *was* the truth? Was it all a game? A sham? What about all those things he said? Plans for the future … plans for another painting … plans for her to be in his life. It was so hard to accept, once again, that she was not wanted.

The train trip back was hell. She wanted a carriage alone but that was impossible. It was after rush hour but still busy with commuters returning home. She was glad she had brought a hat and sunglasses. Despite the fact that the sun was long gone, she hid behind her shades and shut her eyes. She was exhausted.

She longed for her old bedroom, at her mum's, back in Bath. She would plan a trip home in the next few weeks if she could get away. The image soothed her. She grasped hold of a memory of the garden in the summer. She focused on the colour, the scents, the way the wind rustled the leaves in the tree. The branches would brush against her window. When it was warm, she used to fling it open, and the breeze would rush by her cheek and play with her hair. Lulled by the rhythm of the train, she dozed. She was surprised when it pulled into the station.

The college courts were dark, illuminated by only a few lights in the corners. She was walking quickly towards her room when a voice called her out of the gloom.

"Hey, Isa, Isa … not so fast!"

She knew that voice. Her heart lurched in her chest. All at once, she longed for the comfort of Simon's friendship. The unshakable loyalty of his commitment. Isabella turned around.

He was close enough to see her face in the gloom. "Hey … you've been crying. Are you okay? What's …?"

He broke off as she collapsed into his arms and held on to him as if she were drowning.

Hampstead, London N8
25th May

Bella,

I cannot stay silent any longer. Those hours we spent together gave me such great joy, the deepest I have ever felt in my life. I thought I could go on without you but I was wrong. I'm a jerk for not writing before now – it was the coward's way and I'm conscious of it. I appeal to you only to listen to what I have to say. Then it is up to you.

I need to tell you a story. It is one with a chapter that is old, and a chapter that is new.

I was very arrogant when I was young. Maybe you think I still am! Well, it is true in some ways. I know that I often seem very selfish and self-centred. In the beginning, I was very taken up with what Freddie could offer, despite the fact that I was very loud spoken about rejecting all of the status and financial power that my own parents had. Hypocrite, you say? Perhaps. Well, as time showed, I was not authentic or genuine in my protestations. I took the easy way out. I went for what I knew. It made me feel safe, though it also made me feel trapped. I hated myself for caving in. I let Freddie do what she does so well – take control. She ran the household and the children. Of course, she ran me too. She owned me.

I don't say all this to play the martyr. I was not the victim of some vicious plot. I know I have to take responsibility for the decisions I myself made, which brings me to the next part of the story.

Freddie's sexuality was – is – in a word, ambiguous. These days they say fluid. She likes men and women, singles, groups ... photographing, participating, watching ... whenever, whatever. The more outrageous, the better. I was very unclear about my own sexuality when we met. I thought I might be gay, but growing up in my era in Australia, it wasn't even to be considered, let alone disclosed. When she fell pregnant and we were married, it wasn't so bad. Freddie adored me, and my ego just lapped it up. I was swept up in all the games she played – I played right along. A special bond formed between us, rooted in the bedroom. It fed our creativity. My painting was inspired! If I struck a bargain with the devil, it was paying off.

Freddie was possessive, but she became bored very quickly. She was only really aroused when something different was happening, something surprising ... or someone surprising. So, we made a pact. We were allowed to stray, but if she, or I, found someone with special qualities, then we agreed the other could participate.

At first, it was a whirlwind – for years! For a while, it seemed there was someone new every week – always a flavour of the month. We fed on them, and on each other, artistic vampires. But such a frenzy wasn't sustainable. When you met me, I was in a deep ennui ... I wasn't painting, I wasn't living. Freddie and I hated the sight of each other. We had nothing to offer one another except bitterness and resentment. We put a face on for the children, who I daresay have been with their grandparents and at boarding school so much that they cannot tell what lies beneath. I would have left. But where would I have gone? What would be the point? I threw myself into projects, like the Fitz.

But that brings me to the new chapter. To you. You lit me up. You made me come alive again, feel passion beyond anything I'd ever experienced. I was in drought, and you saved me.

She went berserk when she saw your painting. When you see it, you will understand. The inspiration you gave me resulted in a masterpiece, and I am not being conceited when I say so. The energy and sexuality in the piece is astounding. And it is all because of you. Of course, Freddie saw that. She immediately wanted to be included in our relationship.

For the first time in my life with her, I did not want to share. I felt so strongly that what we had, even though it had only been a few weeks, was so special I did not want her to intrude on it. She threatened to cut me off – when I had just started to produce great work again! I decided to give you up all together rather than subject you to her – to our twisted reality.

I never meant to deceive you. I thought that I could keep you for myself, without her knowledge. Selfish again, and self-deceiving. She always did uncover my secrets. I didn't know what to do. What your feelings must have been, I can only imagine. Only know that it was torture for me. Did you feel it too?

I cannot stay away from you. I cannot lose you. And so, this letter. I need to see you. To gaze at your painting and remember our time together is not enough. I try to paint more of you, but it isn't enough – I need the living, breathing, perfect embodiment of passion before me.

We can figure something out so that we can be together. Only forgive me for these past weeks – they have been a wasteland. Can we start over? Let us meet at Kew again, like we talked about. Let me paint you by the magnolia as we planned.

If nothing else, let me at least apologize in person. I am coming to Cambridge to the Fitzwilliam next Wednesday.

Tell me I may see you? Somewhere?
J.

CHAPTER FIFTEEN

Isabella again stood across from his house, in the twilight, shielded by the trees.

What was she doing, hiding in the gloom, snooping in the shadows? She was drawn to their home uncontrollably, helpless as a moth. She shied away from the word stalking – too many false, ugly connotations. He had brought her to the doorstep with his words as effectively as if he'd physically dragged her there.

If anything, she was spying. But *was* this what stalking felt like? Uneasy excitement coursed through her, a fluttering in her stomach, wetness between her thighs. Nervousness akin to arousal. She'd played spying games as a child. An elusive memory drifted forth from the back of her mind. Hide and seek in semi-darkness. Furtive touching and running away. But who were the players? She had been watching someone. Her little sister … in a hallway, behind half-closed doors. Why was this connection with Joshua dredging up old, almost forgotten childhood memories?

Voices and light erupted from a door opening across the street. She startled, heart thumping wildly.

But it wasn't Joshua's – it was his neighbour's. She bundled herself back further into the shadows.

Imagine if it had been Joshua and Freddie leaving the house! But wasn't that why she was here? To catch a glimpse of one or the other of them, or them together? She had no letter in her hand this time. No excuse.

Had *his* letter been a thinly veiled invitation to join them? Why tell her these things if not inviting her in in some way? The very idea of being offered up as some bizarre tribute to their marriage! And if not inviting her to partake in their strange intrigue, he was inviting her to flaunt it with him. To flaunt his wife. Was he being over-dramatic, or was to do so to risk his ruin? He was a grown man – could he really not work out some way to support himself without her, or was it just an excuse to stay in the lap of luxury, nothing to do but paint and suffer his existential angst and fuck strangers he lured back to his home?

Isabella's hands curled into fists, her nails biting into the palms of her hands. She shivered slightly.

Freddie's face was branded on her brain from the photographs. Who was this woman? Who was she to have such a hold over him – financial, familial … sexual? He was in bondage to her. Isabella shivered again, not from the cold.

She wanted to get a sighting of Freddie. Through the window, stepping out the door – it didn't matter. If Joshua's aim had been to whet her curiosity, it was whet. What if she just marched over there and confronted them both?

Just as she took half a step forward, the door opened, and Joshua walked down the steps. He went through the gate, jiggling keys in his hand. Isabella froze, regardless of her intentions just a second before. Moving to open the driver's door of a blue BMW parked on the street, he paused and raised his head. Steeling herself, Isabella emerged from the shadows. "Bella! What–? What a wonderful surprise! What are you doing here? I'm coming up in two days …"

She refused to smile back at him. "Yes, I got your letter. I know ..."

He seemed to recover himself and moved towards her. "Come inside! I'm on my own."

"No!" she said, jerking back. "I didn't come for that. I just need to talk to you, sort out some things. I didn't want to do this in Cambridge. I feel freer to leave here."

"What do you mean? You just got here. Let's have some wine. We can talk inside, light the fire, get comfy."

"No, not there. Let's just go to a quiet bar or café."

Joshua raised his arms in a gesture of defeat.

The pub was open around the corner, not yet busy with the dinner time rush. They ordered a glass of wine each.

"Bella, I'm so glad you're here," Joshua exclaimed. "I actually wanted to tell you something. I wish you'd have come in. Maybe when we've talked, you'll come back with me – to see your painting! We've been so excited – "

He was like a hyper, little boy, acting as though nothing had come between them. Isabella took it all in stunned silence, her hand tight around her wine glass. She sat rigidly in her chair, trying to control her breathing.

"Anyway, we had a party, the first we've had for years and years. And at the party, one of our old friends, an art dealer, made his way uninvited to the studio. He was prying. He apologized for snooping, but then said how bowled over he was when he saw the painting. So now it is the talk of the town, and I am famous – well, not really, but it is a beginning! And it's all because of you."

This couldn't be for real. "Joshua … Really?" her voice caught, 'We' this, and 'we' that! Nothing! For weeks! And then your letter? And then this? I'm glad for you that the painting's going well. That you've done something you're pleased with. I am. It sounds pretty amazing. But I'm a person! Not just a painting. Not just someone who posed for you. A person – with feelings. Are you *that* self-involved?" Isabella broke off, panting, she felt the burning behind her eyes, the dead giveaway that tears were on their way.

Joshua sat gazing into her face, watching her mouth as she spoke. His fingers ran restlessly around his glass. He should have thought that he'd lost her, should have been at her feet begging her forgiveness, but he only cared about his painting. He was clearly impatient to get her back to the house – to sleep with her, surely, but it seemed more to admire his work, his genius. The talk of the town! Her image! What did he expect – for her to be *grateful* to be used that way?

"My darling, please … I'm sorry. I know I hurt you. That's why, in my letter, I tried to explain! When Freddie found out about you, I just wanted to protect you from that side of things." He reached out and blanketed her hand in his. "You are so beautiful … Your face in this light, the shadows, the highlights – this is how I want to paint you. I have been starving for the sight of you! Every time I see you, I want to paint you in just that way. You are magnificent enough that a thousand paintings couldn't capture it!"

"Can you just focus on something other than your art for one minute?" She snatched her hand from under his. "You knew I would be back … didn't you?"

He grinned sheepishly.

She banged her palm against the table. "Well, I don't want to be such a pushover, so predictable. You can't get me so easily. I feel engulfed, drowning, as if I'm losing myself. I got so upset over your disappearing act … and then finding out it was because of Freddie! I can't go on like this."

At least she'd wiped the grin from his mouth. He stared at her earnestly now.

"I know, my dearest, I know. But it is all so –"

"Complicated, difficult, yes. I know. Can you just stop and think about how all this impacts me? I'm so mixed up. I don't know what to do. I wasn't going to respond. I wasn't going to meet you at the Fitz. I was going to make *you* wait."

"And I would have!" Joshua interrupted. "I would wait for you until I couldn't bear it any longer. But then I would find you. I found you once – I would do so again. I told you I want you in my life."

"I wrote you a letter you don't know about. I was here before, about to put it through the letterbox, but then I realized all those people were gathered at your house, when you weren't even meant to be home … there was music, the windows were open and I could hear laughing, the house all lit up. That must have been the night you had your party. I imagined you and Freddie together, so happy. I couldn't stand it. You say in your letter you decided to do without me? Well, I made that decision too! I promised myself I would never see you again."

She stopped, choked and breathless.

He was very still. "But you changed your mind."

"There you go again, jumping to conclusions. It would suit you, wouldn't it? You could go on just as before. No change needed. And I have to be the one to suck it up and accept everything. You lied to me! You and Freddie have something together, and I'm just the bit on the side."

To her shame, Isabella began to feel that her burning eyes were about to give way and the tears flow over.

"Hold on, hold on, now."

She lifted her chin and met his gaze. As though someone had switched on a light, it seemed Joshua was finally in the room with her. The fascinating, caring, magical man she'd met on the train had returned. Isa could see right through him as she looked deep into his eyes. She felt all the anger bleed out of her. This gaze, like a light beaming on her, was the very thing. The connection. She gasped. But the danger. She felt herself at risk of being lost once more.

She gave herself a mental shake. Remembering. This was his life. He wanted to make his dreams come true. That art critic was so impressed. He was on another roll. He may think he just needed to be patient, be more loving, make her feel special. And Freddie? Could he manage Freddie?

"Oh Bella, please, please. No tears. Here." He reached over and gently wiped a tear from her cheek. "Don't end it. Never end it. It's not like you say. With Freddie. With us. We can work this out."

Isabella looked up at him. His face looked ravaged and grey, in stark contrast to the excited boy who'd greeted her, who'd tried to share his joy with her. Her stomach turned over. She'd wanted to confront him, annihilate him, and she had. Was she happy now? Could she walk away?

"We need to talk more about you and Freddie. And what is happening in the now. Not so much about the past. I can accept the reasons you gave for how you got together and why it has continued. I understand about the children, and your career. But

I would have thought that you could make it on your own, especially given how good you are."

He caught up her hands in his, and this time she didn't pull away. "That's what I've been thinking! That if things go well from now on, then being on my own could be possible … but not yet. Things are still too iffy. I need to be surer that I have something secure. Please, be patient. I've hurt you. But we have something. It's too precious to lose. I was a fool to try and deny it and I put you through hell in the process. I won't push you to come back with me. You need time to consider – I know it. But from now, you will have perfect honesty from me. Please. Give me a chance to make it up to you."

She returned the pressure of his fingers. She couldn't trust him yet. But the idea of following through and never seeing him again? It was too much to bear. She'd been deluding herself, hence ending up outside his house. She'd needed him to actually look her in the eye and promise her there was something to save, something to make this madness worthwhile.

She took a deep breath. "Okay."

His eyes had misted over. He gave her a tremulous smile. Here and now, she didn't doubt that he truly cared. But when they were apart? When he was with *her*?

"You're right though – I do need some time. I've been so lost … I need to find myself."

"And when you do?"

She smiled at him shyly. "When I do … I'll meet you under the magnolia."

Parting at the entrance to the tube, they sealed it with a kiss.

CHAPTER SIXTEEN

"So, how did it go? When are you going to do the Kew paint?" Freddie tapped her foot on the floor of the studio. "Come on, come on, answer me."

"I don't know. I don't know. Oh just get off my back and leave me alone!" Joshua whirled around from his easel pointing his brush threateningly right at Freddie's face.

"Whoa, huh, hey.. watch it sonny. I don't care for that look in your eye. I come back here after a few days away and here you are still, almost in exactly the same place as when I left. Something must have happened. You must have seen her..." she broke off as Joshua took another step towards her. She quickly changed tack. Freddie did not want to push him too far. She took a step back, conceding some ground. "Now Josh, darling. You know we have a deal. You don't need me to remind you, do you?"

"Oh Christ, cut that treacly tone. There's no need for it. Remind me! That's all you ever do these days. And for your information, I don't even know if there will be a Kew paint. I certainly don't know when."

"What … you, losing the velvet touch?"

"For God's sake. She went off back to Cambridge in a huff, okay? She's all upset. Upset about you, if you must know."

Freddie sat, enjoying the moment. At last, she had a chance to feel something. What was it? Satisfaction? Revenge? Joshua was clearly very put out this morning. No sign of the lady in question in the studio. Except of course for the work. That item of exquisite magnificence was still on an easel against the wall. But the preliminary sketches for Kew seemed piled in the corner, not displayed as they were before she left. *I wonder... she mused to herself.*

All the way back in the train she had wondered what she would find. Deliberately she had given Joshua no notice of her return. What had she hoped? To find them 'in flagrante'? That would have been delicious, yes, but not wise for any longer-term goals she had. Hmm, she had to be more patient, move slowly to get her prize.

"Okay, okay, I'll back off, for now." She adopted a sincere, conciliatory tone. "I don't mean any harm. I just feel left out. And some of our best times were when we were in it together. I want to be part of it again somehow. But not to ruin it for you." Freddie gave him a wobbly smile. "Please?"

"Wow. It's been a long, long time since I heard you say please. Since you wanted anything from me."

Freddie's tone rose again. "Well, I'm not going to beg."

"Okay, okay" he conceded.

"I wrote to her. I've seen her – but nothing happened. She needed her feathers stroking. She needs some time. It's been absolute hell. I can't paint, I'm not moving forward. My old stuff is rubbish. To have had that burst of inspiration again and then have it yanked away…I can't sleep, I come in here and just pace, or clean brushes."

He broke off and as if to prove a point started pacing around the studio his brush and cleaning rag clenched in a tight fist. "Maybe there was some progress yesterday, we met for a drink."

He glanced towards Freddie who was gazing at him with a smirk on her lips and a question in her eye. "No, she didn't come here, no sex, nothing like that. That part might all be gone, over…" his voice caught.

"Oh my goodness, no wonder you look so miserable." Freddie stopped just short of cutting sarcasm, she reminded herself to hold on to being the comforting, listening wife as long as she could. History had taught her well that she was only successful when she walked that line skilfully between irate parent and supportive friend. She knew her emotional power, she was good at keeping him on his toes.

She continued more silkily, "I can see that this seems all pretty desperate right now. But I doubt that all is lost. You'll think of something." She finished, wanting to be upbeat, provide encouragement for his flailing ego.

Joshua did another circuit, his pace slowing, his breathing more regular. He looked up and a small smile creased the side of his mouth. "We – ell, just maybe."

Stopping he took a long look out the window, the late morning sun shone on his masterpiece in the corner. The colours glowed, shimmered. The forms danced, twirled. His smile broadened.

Freddie wondered what he was thinking – something about *her* she assumed. His voice took on the warm low note that accompanied happier thoughts, at the beginning of arousal. Freddie knew that sign, though it had been an age since it was in response to her. Joshua's mood seemed to shift; his tone lightened.

"I'll let you know if the Kew paint happens. Or maybe not if, but when. Umm, er," stuttering now as he thought it through, "m- ma- maybe you can go earlier and s - set yourself up where it would be impossible to be seen?" His voice rose as a question and sat drifting in the air, as if buoyed up by the sunbeam. A beam which had moved now to shine directly on Joshua's head.

Freddie stood slowly and turned to leave but just caught a glimpse of how the light haloed his hair. Aha! That angelic younger side of Joshua always managed to draw some tenderness from her. It was the vulnerability. It made her feel needed.

So many good memories of that distant past when they were both so much younger. And crazy. She missed all that. Motherhood was all very well to keep up appearances and all but really, she had always doubted she was cut out for it. Thank God for boarding schools. And her parents. Quite apart from the money, they were good to the girls. Yes, those girls, they were growing up. But not quite fast enough. She looked forward to when they were old enough to really do the great things that mattered, less hockey sticks and horses and more travel, exhibitions, the opera. She imagined that they would be quite good companions for travelling. There were all the indications they were bright, would bring interesting diversions into her life. But not quite the diversions she really had in mind. *That* side of her life she would always keep absolutely private.

Freddie left the studio with a pursed smile compressing her lips and a twinkle in her eye that Joshua could not see. Her thoughts swirled. She revelled in her victory. So, he will paint her after all, and I will be there to see it! *We shall see what we shall see*, she thought, *and in the meantime, I will try harder to be all sweetness and light.*

Hampstead, London N8
June 15

My dearest,

I have stayed away. I have been trying to give you time. But no more. Please, please, come to Kew. I have enclosed one of my drawings. All I have to do is to work out the best bit, which is you. I have just sketched you in from memory, but it's not right, I need the real you to be there. I have been to the spot, our spot, our special place by the magnolia, many times this month. My sketch book is full. But it is also empty. As is my heart without you.

I hope you are not still mad. I hope I am a little bit forgiven?
You must know how sorry I am I was such a beast.

By way of a peace offering, I wondered whether you would let me take you out? Join me for an art opening? It would be lovely for us to do something together. The Courtauld is having a Schiele retrospective and I have tickets...not formal, just a drink or two and I would just love to see your reaction to his work – there is a promise of some lesser known ones from a private collection that has just been sold. We could meet there about 4pm and have a little dinner after? Please, please say yes...

Missing you, my love,
J.

CHAPTER SEVENTEEN

Isabella unrolled the sketch. It was a watercolour tint. So subtle, so fresh. Her face was quite recognizable, whatever Joshua might say, her hair flowing behind her shoulders, gleaming with reddish lights. Her head was tilted back, and throat exposed, as were her breasts. They were bared almost completely, just covered across the nipples with a pale, pastel-coloured shawl, the long fringe hanging down beside her thigh, which was just visible through an almost sheer skirt.

The drawing was incomplete below the hip line, just a rough sketch to show scale. The detail was in the face and the shoulders to the waist. She looked at herself as though looking at a stranger, amazed at the idea that this was her. The watercolour was of a very beautiful woman. Not young, not a nubile innocent. She stood there with confidence, holding her ground, throwing her head back, aware, but not fully aware, of her power. And it was not just a sexual power, but a sensual one. The head was tilted but the face turned so the eyes looked straight at the viewer. In the eyes she could see the maturity and experience of her years.

'Wow, thought Isabella. *He did get it. He has captured it – my age.*

She had thought he might idealize her when he painted, make her young and perfect her body. It had been a reason for her hesitation. But this was an older woman. And she was beautiful. If this was his idea of a sketch, what did the canvas hold?

Isabella re opened the letter, more gently this time as she had knowledge now of its content and tone. She smiled to herself. A rather self - contented grin.

Hmm, I have him just a little bit on the run. Isa read the part again about the invitation. To be able to go out, in public, like a date! This was what she had been waiting for. If he is prepared to out himself with her on his arm, then there was some progress after all. And the Freddie factor? Well, let's leave that for another day to consider.

She felt warmed, touched by the tender side of Joshua. Hopeful that he was really changing his spots and not just being nicer to achieve his own ends.

"So, I see a letter for Cambridge on the hall table… back to love and romance?" Freddie tried hard to keep the bitter edge out of her voice, she smirked at Joshua, "Care to tell? That's if you won't show?"

"I have written to Isa suggesting Kew again…so, happy?" Joshua glanced briefly at his wife over his newspaper, not sure at all what mood she was in this morning.

"You wrote that one without me standing over you…huh!" Freddie scoffed, "Wonder what else you are keeping from me."

"Oh Freddie, Freddie, Freddie, you do take on so. I know you want in. I know we have a deal." Joshua dropped the strident tone and spoke more softly, looking directly into Freddie's eyes, "I am trying to make it all work, for all of us, please bear with me."

His approach worked as Freddie visibly calmed down, she sat next to him, and placed her hand on his thigh. Squeezing gently and running her fingers up towards his crotch she put on her sweetest tone,

"And just what do you have in mind. Tell me. Give me the blow by blow as it gives me something delicious to think on."

Joshua took a deep breath, "There is something I have in mind. I see you are a bit calmer so I will fill you in – though nothing is decided yet, I have just floated the idea."

"What, what, details please. I want details. When will the paint be, and where at Kew. Tell me… tell me, how marvellous, I was thinking about where I would hide and what I would see, and how it would be, seeing her, and being so close. But so far. Delicious." Freddie, breathless, sprung up and started pacing, humming to herself with excitement.

"Whoa hold on, hold on, th… this um… is not exactly about Kew." Joshua stuttered nervously, "I er

I just wanted to say that I um er have tickets for that Schiele opening… and I thought…"

"Yes, yes, great. Let's do that. We haven't been out together in a long, long time." Freddie interrupted him. She plunked down again next to him, gripping his upper thigh, returning to the squeezing and stroking.

Joshua shifted awkwardly, and her hand dropped away.

"What… what?" Freddie reacting to his withdrawal, sensed something was up, her tone started to rise again, "You are keeping something back...no… no! I don't believe it!" Freddie glared at him, breathing hard and clicking her fingernails on the tabletop with impatience.

"Umm yes, how well you know me. I am thinking that if I asked Isa to come, it would be a good way to make up, to get her on side… so then she would be sure to say yes to Kew." He stumbled over his words, his tone sheepish, he was starting to sweat. He had hoped she would be calm enough to hear his plan... but a bit of a miscalculation. Her jealousy, it seems knows no bounds.

Freddie's mind was in a whirlwind. What was he doing? Was he seriously thinking he could outwit her. Take Isabella, in public, to a show, as if *they* were the couple. Sure, many people knew that things had not been great between them for a while, and they had not been seen out together, but if Joshua were to be seen with this beauty, then the cat would be out of the bag. How would she manage the rumour mill then when it got up and running.

There was no way she was going to lose control of this. It was going to happen *her* way, or not at all.

Freddie tossed her head and folded her arms, and leaning in towards him she hissed, "Ok we'll all go."

Joshua balked, his face paling, "No way! Isa would never agree."

"We won't tell her; I'll just show up!" Freddie warmed to the ridiculousness of this notion, her imagination already playing pictures of the three together.

Joshua spluttered, "And you think then you will have a chance to woo her into our little menage? Don't be stupid, that approach will just push her further away. You have to keep your eye on the higher prize. Wait, be more patient and I will bring her to you."

"My, my, who now is showing a greater finesse in strategy, to lure, and ensnare the precious treasure." Freddie purred, "OK go, go with her, but mind you introduce her as your new model, nothing more, and those who know me there must be told I am joining you later for dinner."

Joshua raised his eyebrows, "But…you won't..."

"No, not this time. But be warned," she almost spat, "I will have friends there who shall be watching."

"Yes, I am sure your spies will report back." Joshua shook out his newspaper hiding his disgust from Freddie.

"And one more thing. Bring her back here." Freddie was relentless. "I am sure she would like to see your latest painting. And then there are the others to show her in my room," she jutted her chin, "I will go and visit the parents and see our girls."

Freddie, blissfully unaware that Isabella had already seen her room, smoothly unwound herself from the chair where her legs and arms were wrapped. Sighing, and smiling that secret smile, she glided from the kitchen. She savoured her thoughts about what might come later. Joshua being seen with Isa was a small price to pay for the chance of post gallery entertainment. And more good may just come out of it for the art world to be presented with this luscious creature. The value of the painting just went way up!

CHAPTER EIGHTEEN

On the train heading for London, Isabella wondered if it had all been inevitable. She smiled to herself. She might have held out for a while, but he was just so magnetic. And the idea of going on a date, almost like a real couple, was so beguiling. Irresistible.

His letter represented another turn around. On reflection there had been so many about faces that she was getting dizzy! But this time, this time, she hoped things were settling into something she could count on. The watercolour was amazing. She was very tempted to do the modelling for him at Kew. But she had not quite decided. Tonight, would be the test of whether she could trust him enough.

There was something about the modelling and the intensity of his gaze, she was just now starting to realize. This was the core to her vulnerability. It was completely disarming, the ultimate intimacy in a way – even more than physical sex. If she could trust him, then it was the core of a positive connection for her. And therefore, the key she sought for the ultimate in relationship. But if not, it would become the polar opposite. Being disarmed without trust was akin to violation, rape.

Isabella was only very peripherally aware that she was getting close to the interior of her fixation on this man. What indeed had driven her to have many relationships in the past which had all foundered. It was being the object of their adoration. This was her fix.

She had dressed carefully. She knew she looked amazing. However, she still would like Joshua to say so. Her black dress was plain except for two startling features. The very features that convinced her to buy it, despite it being way beyond her budget. There was a surprising panel of sequins in the skirt that only showed when she walked or if she stood with her hip and leg positioned in a particular way to optimize the reveal. She grinned, this relationship with Joshua is all about reveal!

The second feature was the deep plunging back neckline, almost to her waist. Again, only revealed if she removed or adjusted the embroidered shawl she had carefully draped over her shoulders. The shawl was the very one Joshua had painted in the watercolour. The one planned for the Kew paint. It was even more exquisite than the quick sketch portrayed. Antique silk. The fabric was so soft and smooth, light as a feather as it brushed her skin, and the embroidered colours were muted and pale with age but still beautiful. The tiny precise stitches made stunning swirls of patterning of exotic birds and butterflies.

It had been such a shock and delight to open the parcel. It arrived soon after she sent her note of acceptance to Joshua last week. How amazing, it just poured like liquid silver from the packet to form a rippled pool on the floor of the Porters Lodge. If she had had any idea of the contents, she would never have opened it there. Attracted quite the attention she recalled giggling to herself. Oh well, let them gossip, and fantasize. What with them all knowing she was studying Cleo, and now receiving exotic gifts by mail, who knows how she may entertain them next?

Arriving outside the gallery Isa had a flashback to that first time, at the National Portrait Gallery. She assumed then that Joshua would be waiting upstairs but he had surprised her by being in the foyer. And this evening, after she passed the bubbling ankle and knee level fountains that lined the courtyard, he surprised her again. Where was he? She mounted the high curved staircase, marvelling at the Georgian blue colour scheme, the wrought iron and gilt and then, at the top, all those small intimate gallery rooms.

Joshua was standing in the late afternoon light gazing, seemingly transfixed, at a painting of two naked women embracing.

"Hello, my darling, it seems like such a long time." Joshua tore his gaze from the painting and looked at Isabella with similar longing. He kissed both her cheeks, gripping her shoulders.

"Well, if this painting is anything like the rest of the exhibition it will be intriguing." She replied with a wide smile. Isa was still a little breathless, from the stairs, from seeing Joshua, and confronting the subject of this painting. "Is this typical? And how are you by the way?" The usual pleasantries of greeting seemed irrelevant when Isa looked more widely around the room.

"This room has been reserved for his most erotic drawings and paintings. They are mainly of his lover of many years. He did however have ongoing fantasies about women together. This one of his lover and wife. It was a way of trying to reconcile how he could be with them both." Joshua was looking at Isa out of the corner of his eye as his words took on a serious quality. She gasped, looking again more closely at the painting.

"Hmm, seems the subject and maybe even the pose is quite close to home huh?" Isa tried a teasing tone.

"Well yes, there is that. Quite the co-incidence that this is on right now while I am having my own muddle." Joshua linked arms with Isa and smiled into her eyes.

"Yes." She thought, "A muddle for sure, but then, just maybe, everything will be alright."

Her confidence continued to be boosted by Joshua's manner towards her. Any introductions were brief, and Isa was described as a friend whom he was trying to convince to be his new model. He neatly sidestepped queries about Freddie, placing her in 'the country' as the children were on half term. The paintings were amazing, Isabella was blown away. A great range of religious subjects, land and townscapes, but she declared the nudes and erotic portraits as her favourites.

Joshua was quiet on their way back to his home following their intimate, al fresco meal. They went by taxi and his arm was loosely around her shoulders. He seemed relaxed, murmuring softly into her ear, placing delicate soft kisses on the back of her neck and along her hairline. Isa was not absolutely sure what was to happen next. It had not been discussed. But there did seem to be an assumption unfolding. An inevitability.

"Need I say again just how beautiful you are, and how that shawl is fantastic on you, stunning. I just knew it would be." His hand stroked the smooth flesh of her neck, and his fingers began to tickle down her back, touching delicately each vertebra and making tiny circles as he moved lower. "Wow," he whispered breathlessly, "such a magnificent back, and it goes so far down and down, to there and there. "He broke off, now silently exploring inside the back neckline of her dress. Her mind followed his fingers, willing them to explore lower, wondering how far he would go in the taxi.

She knew by his breathing that he was aroused. That the bulge in his pants as he pressed against her hip was his invitation. No words, no discussion. Should she be angry yet again and hurt that this is him making assumptions and taking her for granted. The big Use?

But no, she knew she could stop this at any time, get out, go back to Cambridge. She was just as much a willing participant as she sat serenely beside him. It all seemed to fit, just right. Her voice was low and throaty, but calm, relaxed, almost a purr, "Hmm that feels so wonderful. I have so missed your touch."

"There will be plenty more where this came from. Will you spend the night with me?

We will be all alone. We can have the full run of the place. I do so need to show you that I am sorry, and I want to make it up to you. Let me love you."

The slow cadence of his speech matched the dance of his fingers as they moved lower beneath her dress. His quick inhale of breath told Isa that he had discovered no underwear. His hand cupped the top of her bottom as his little finger slid in the cleft, searching, searching. She was wet, hot. Isa shifted her hips to widen the gap, her own breathing beginning to match the increased pace of his.

"My, my, my, you seem to have forgotten something," Isa just caught his tiny whisper. Another reminder of another time. She recalled that train ride, which took her memory back to Kew, a topic still to be resolved. Regardless, it felt so great to have some history with this man, despite the fact that they had only met a few months ago.

CHAPTER NINETEEN

The house was artistically lit, a few lamps here and there, warmly welcoming. The entryway filled with the scent of lilies. Isa slipped off her shoes, determined to try to feel comfortable in Freddie's home.

"I know when we last met at the pub you said all I ever speak about is my art. I am so excited to show you the painting I can hardly stand it, but I want you to know that I can wait, it's up to you." Joshua's words came out in a rush, his hand rubbing the back of his neck and pulling at his earlobe.

"What's this, you seem jittery all of a sudden… are you sure we are here alone? Is it Freddie?" Isa wondered if this was some kind of trap. But as Joshua moved towards her with his arms outstretched, she dismissed that niggling thought.

"No, no, everything's fine. I-I just was not sure h-how you would feel being back here. That's all. What about a drink?"

The studio felt familiar to Isabella. She realized that she had missed it.

"I have a foolish urge to dance again. Must be the turpentine smell. Goes right to my head", she laughed lightly as she went through the doorway. "Oh my…

wow… it - it's am – amazing." More words failed her as Isa caught sight of the painting, lit now as Joshua turned on the overhead spot.

She stood completely still, her turn to be transfixed by art. Her thoughts whirled. Was that really her? The overlapping limbs, swirling hair, tilted faces. And the colour! The entire spectrum of the rainbow was there, in every shade and every tint. As if connected to a puppeteer's string, Isa's head gently moved back and forth in time with the imaginary dancing figures.

Joshua gazed at her, closely watching her every reaction. He smiled and moved closer.

"I can see you like it," he murmured softly and kissed the top of her head.

"Oh yes, it's magical."

They came together then as if they had never been apart. As if there was no muddle. As if they belonged. The fit, as Isa termed it. They held each other for a long time. Just holding, breathing each other in. Their bodies aligned as they stood close, Isa's head cradled into Joshua's shoulder, not yet ready to tear her gaze from the painting.

"So, my darling, what now… shall we go to bed?"

"Oh, um…" she hesitated, "Not quite ready for that. I want to prolong the joy. What about a game? The dancing figures have me thinking. You deserve another fix of me performing. What about it?" Isa nibbled Joshua's ear and blew into it gently. "But not here, I've done that. Where else can I dance for you, I wonder?"

Isabella considered again what she had been plotting. At first just a whim, not even embellished enough to be a fantasy. Now, emboldened by the painting and the power it seemed to give her, she thought again about her desire to take some control of this place, this house, this home that was Freddie's. To make her mark. To make a piece of it hers, if only for a short time, and yes, she admitted to herself, to get her own back. And where then would be the best place for that? Her mind turned to what she had found in Freddie's room – her lair. Perfect!

She giggled low in her throat and grasped his hand, "I want to treat you. Come with me."

Isa led Joshua by the hand along the hall in the direction of his bedroom.

"I thought you weren't ready for…" he broke off, wrinkling his brow.

"No, we aren't going in there, not yet." She stood before the door she remembered to be Freddie's bedroom – noting the shocked look on Joshua's face.

"What?" He gasped, "In here?"

"Why not? You said we could have the run of the house." Her voice rang with new confidence.

"Yes, but… maybe not…" Joshua ended weakly, following her into the darkened room.

Taken by surprise as the light went on in her bedroom beyond the closet, Freddie just managed to quickly turn hers off behind the mirror to avoid detection. She sat in her hiding place, amazed, stunned, to see the very object of her fantasy out there in her room, cavorting in front of Joshua. As she listened to Isabella rummage through the coat hangers and shelves, Freddie felt a rising rage, aware that this wench must have been here before, had ransacked through her stuff. She was clearly looking for something specific right now. Freddie became breathless. The sweating started. She was wet under her arms and between her thighs. She felt the back of her shirt, wet, sticking to her hot skin.

Utterly irate, she jumped up, trembling with how she had been violated, her private sanctum breached. About to burst through into the room, she stopped short, making the huge effort required to calm herself.

Now now get a grip. She talked herself down silently inside her head. *Act like that and you'll screw it all up…*

My god, just what is she up to? What kind of creature is this?

Freddie had the impression from Joshua that, although an older woman, but far from elderly in her beauty, energy and wit, Isa was a tender-hearted soul, sensitive and, for Joshua and Freddie in their predatory roles, an easy mark to lure and dominate. Freddie had misjudged this Isabella. Intrigued now, Freddie settled in her favourite easy chair to watch the show, video camera at the ready.

Isa humming to herself, gestured for Joshua to sit as she bade him to close his eyes. She had found what she was searching for in the closet.

What Freddie saw unfold was better than her best fantasy. Except for the fact that she could not touch, this was the best voyeuristic view through a keyhole that one could ever have, in several lifetimes.

The sensuous, curvaceous flesh revealed itself as Isa removed her dress to reveal her uplift half bra, the black lace so sheer and delicate it hardly contained those magnificent full globes that threatened to spill over, the pink nipples now erect with excitement contrasting sharply against the pale creamy skin.

Joshua stirred in his chair. "Now, can I look now?" his tone hoarse, almost strangled.

"No, not yet I'm not ready. Be patient." Isa's humming went up in volume. Joshua and Freddie both recognized the strains of a Can Can dancing tune. *Shades of the Folies Bergere...* whispered Freddie to herself, hardly able to contain her excitement.

Joshua remonstrated, his protest loud but playful, "Patient! How can I wait when I am imagining what you are doing."

Transfixed by that face and hair, which Isa was now twisting and pushing into a black top hat, Freddie had not yet taken time to focus on the rest of her quarry's body. Isa's back was to her as she put her arms through the sleeves of an elegant velvet black tailcoat. It fit her like a glove. The fabric smoothly enveloped the exquisite angle from the curve of her shoulders across and down her back, nipping in at her waist. Isa bent forward a little to remove her half-slip. She slowly turned to check her image in the mirror.

"Fuck!" Freddie gasped aloud, but quickly put her hand over her mouth for fear of discovery. Her eyes darted everywhere, drinking in the stunning vision. That arse, the curve of that hip, the sensuous belly, and above the thigh high black stockings, below the garter belt, and nestled between those suspenders, Freddie gazed adoringly at the very core of her desire. That black thatch, clipped into a vee but still a bush, healthy enough to lace her fingers through and comb, and pull, and tweak, until there were moans of pleasure and begging for more.

The gasps behind the mirror were matched by those in front as Joshua was finally told he could open his eyes. Isabella stood beaming, her hands firmly placed on her hips, as she watched a look of incredulity cross Joshua's face and adoration and lust light up his eyes.

"I said you would get a big surprise. You like then?" She laughed and resumed her Can Can humming, moving her hips in time and beginning to swirl and twirl in a dance. She kicked her legs high in time with her hum, evoking that classically erotic Parisienne image.

"Like, oh my god, you are…" Joshua broke off. No more words were needed. He moved to the front of his chair, restless, impatient, reaching out for her, his tone urgent. "Get over here, come on, come on, please."

"Just a few more twirls, let the anticipation rise, the temptation grow." Isa's dancing song gave way to teasing laughter, and for her grand finale she halted, doffed her hat and with a cheeky grin she bowed. But the bow was away from her audience. As Isabella bent over, the tails of the coat parted and Joshua and Freddie both had a clear view of the curve of her bum and the secret, dark recesses of Isa's magic cleavage.

"Oh god," Joshua groaned, "Come here. I can't stand it. That dominatrix look has always done it for me. All you need are high boots and a whip! Look at the state I'm in. So hard it won't fit in my pants. What am I going do with this wonder?" He undid his flies and out sprang his red bulging cock. It glistened with wetness in the lamplight.

It was Freddie's turn to gasp. *Well – that's unexpected.* It was a pleasure she had not seen in a long while. This woman was a real find to turn him on like that. A benefit to us all.

Isa moved closer and looked directly into Joshua's eyes. "I can do something about that," And with another cheeky grin, right there on the bedroom floor of her lover's wife, the room of her enemy, she knelt down before him. She took his throbbing member into her mouth and sucked, licked and kissed it. She massaged his balls and tickled the penis head with her tongue until Joshua groaned.

"No, no. I don't want to come here, not in Freddie's room. I want to be inside you in my own bed I want you to be all mine."

Hearing these last words broke Freddie from her reverie. It was all she could do to stop herself leaping out of her secret hiding place and scream *No, she's mine, she's mine, and he also, always will be mine.*

Sitting trembling in her chair, her bedroom quiet now and darkened as they had turned off the lights, Freddie tried to take stock.

CHAPTER TWENTY

Isa kissed Joshua gently on his brow. The early morning light was just enough for her to get dressed by and creep towards the door, shoes in hand.

"Wha-what, where are you going?" a sleepy voice from under the covers. "Wha-what's the time?"

"Hi there. I said last night I would have to leave at dawn. I have a lecture on this afternoon. Have to prepare. Can't be missed. Sorry." Her voice was soft, she walked back to the bed.

"Oh." His tone was almost whiney, he pouted, "I just want to snuggle some more and meander, languish all over your body."

"Languish?" she laughed at him, loving this tender, half-awake side of him.

"Hmm… wrong word but right feeling. Kind of a languid ravish."

"Well, another time, soon."

"Yes, we are agreed, right? Kew next week?" Joshua sat up to make his point more clear. "We shall meet at the magnolia?"

"Yes, yes my darling. The magnolia it shall be." She blew kisses from the doorway.

"Huh, finally you emerge." Freddie's tone had a bitter edge. "I was wondering when you would come for your coffee."

"Oh my god, how long have you been here. I hope you didn't..." Joshua's appalled tone and bloodless face told Freddie all she needed to know. He was panicked in case the two women had crossed paths.

"Hmm, panicked huh? We-ell I could tell you we had it out in the front hall, she leaving and me coming in." Freddie smirked as Joshua gaped, eyes wide. "But that would be a lie. You would have heard us. Or I could tell you that I have just arrived. And I saw her in the street going to the train. But that would also be a lie." Freddie settled back into her chair, folding her arms, she was enjoying his discomfort.

"Dammit Freddie, for god's sake answer my question. When did you get here?"

Freddie waited a long moment, relishing her power and her turn in the spotlight. "We-ll we-ll." She repeated her deliberate hesitation, "Umm ... I didn't ever leave."

"Wh-wh-what? "Joshua spluttered, face now flushed, he sank heavily into a chair at the kitchen table. "What are you saying?"

"What does it sound like dummy, not rocket science. I have been here all the time. I didn't go to see the girls after all. I decided that as it was pretty well guaranteed you would bring her back here. And then maybe, just maybe, I might get a glimpse of her. I thought somehow, I could figure I could do it on the sly. Take a peek when you were all distracted in the studio. But then… wow, wowee! You did give me a show. I hadn't asked for all that. I must thank you sometime." Freddie began to growl deep in her throat, as she sat forward looking right at Joshua. She slowly licked her lips.

"Wh –when, wh-what did you…" the stuttering was getting worse.

"Oh Jesus, don't be so pathetic. Spit it out! When did I see her, what did I see? When and what do you think? I was in my most comfortable place, watching the best entertainment I have seen in a long, long time – maybe ever. That is something we really do agree on. She's utterly stunning."

"You were behind your mirror." Realization crossed Joshua's face, "You saw her, you saw us."

"Hmm bingo! Yep. And it was worth it. Hard to stay quiet though and still. That little minx had obviously been in there before. Rooting through my gear. But… the show she put on. It was worth it not to stop her."

"That's not playing fair! I had said you could hide and see her at Kew. But to do it here. Without me knowing… you're the one who keeps droning on about our deal. You have well and truly crossed the line now!"

"I didn't really believe there was going to be a paint at Kew. If I had waited for that I might have been waiting forever. So, I just took it into my own hands. I wanted to see her. I needed to look at this wench of yours. Don't be so angry darling. What I saw was amazing. I want to compliment you on your taste. I didn't hurt anyone. Not you, and definitely not Isabella. She is truly beautiful." Freddie took on a lower, more pleading tone, "Come on darling, settle down. It's just your pride a bit bruised. I must say though that that amazing erection of yours must have been worth it. Huh? Well?" she grinned across at him.

The increased warmth from Freddie, as always, worked its spell on Joshua, and he settled back into his chair as if now prepared to bask in the glory of his find.

"Shall we enter into a little secret plotting and scheming then about your lovely lady? We did agree there would be a sharing."

Gleaning strength from his healing ego Joshua asserted, "Not just yet. No meetings until after the painting is done. Then we'll see. I don't want to jeopardize that."

"Ok, ok, I am fine for now about not meeting her in person. But I do think that we each want and need something from the other. You need my financial and domestic support to make the paintings happen, and I want more of her. Neither of us can be too pissed off at the other. There is a risk she will walk. We will both be losers then. We must work together." Freddie smiled to herself. Her most cajoling tone usually did the trick. "And by the way. Is she your wench now?

Have you charmed her enough that she will model for you?"

"Yes, yes. Kew is on."

"Good, she will be worth a fortune to us. The paintings you will do with her as inspiration and my support. Incredible. There is the money yes, but also, her value to us, our marriage. This is just what we needed. We were getting stale. Just the thing to brighten us up. So, white feather for now? Truce?" Joshua nodded and watched with grudging admiration, and some relief, as Freddie flounced out of the kitchen humming the Can Can.

CHAPTER TWENTY ONE

She found him set up with his easel, almost hidden behind the shrubbery. The high sun cast leafy shadows on the ground. The wind rustled the leaves above gently, and she could hear a robin chirping. The distant thrum of traffic and rumble of a train was so faint it belonged to another world. They could have been anywhere, miles away in the country, not in the middle of a busy park in the middle of one of the busiest cities in the world.

Isabella had worn her sheer skirt, just as Joshua had planned in his sketch. As she walked out into the small clearing, he turned and smiled. As requested, she was wearing the beautiful Chinese silk shawl, the light making the pastel swirls dance on the glistening silver fabric.

Joshua took her face in his hands, bending down to kiss her gently. "I am so, so glad you agreed. And here you are. I can hardly believe it!"

"I am a bit nervous, but this spot looks quite private. Are you sure …?"

"Yes, of course, of course. I have been thinking about this, fantasizing about it, planning it for months. Come over here, just in front of the tree. Did you like my sketch? That's how I want you to stand. Do you think you can manage to get into that pose? And to hold it for a while? Oh, so wonderful, the day is perfect. Hardly any wind. And warm enough I think for ... yes, take off your top, and wrap yourself in the shawl, yes, that's right ..."

Joshua went on and on, breathless, so very excited. Isabella said nothing, not that she could have got a word in. She followed his instructions, quickly infected with his excitement.

"We have light now for a few hours. It won't even take that long, now I have done the sketches. It's just getting the right colours and the tone for your skin and where the sun hits you just right, and the light in your eyes. Yes, hold back your head, brush your hair back and look around at me … yes, yes!"

Isabella stood in the pose she remembered from the sketch. She wrapped the shawl over her bare arms and draped it just over the top of her breasts, the fringes and tassels hanging way, way down. Such a beautiful shawl, admiring it in the sunlight, stunning. She breathed deeply, relaxing into the setting. She smiled to herself.

"Yes, yes, that's right, think relaxed, happy, wonderful memories. We have just made love and you have had a wonderfully powerful orgasm. A knowing little grin, like a secret, and a warm, loving light in your eyes. Look at me and remember. Recall the feeling. Feel it again in your mind, in your body. Where do you feel it in your body? Where are my hands going? Where am I kissing … licking … nibbling … sucking? I see you are doing as you are told. What a good girl you are. You are very good at imagining. I can see what is happening to your nipples, and the pink flush down your throat and across your chest. Very, very sexy."

Isabella was beginning to enjoy this, the semi-public setting, Joshua's fixed attention, his words up and down her spine, doing delicious things to her body. There was the risk of someone seeing, a family strolling by. But the park seemed empty, this section of the gardens very quiet. Just that bird still making his presence known and the wind gently lifting her skirt.

She shifted a little to stretch her back and tilted her face briefly to ease her neck. *What was that?*

A glint of light blinded her for a second, as if the sun had reflected off something. Just her imagination? No, there it was again – a flash.

"Joshua! I think there's someone …"

Freddie cursed the cramp that was settling into her calf. It was all very well to be there early, but it was no easy task to hold herself still for so long.

"Set yourself up," Joshua had said. "Take a blanket. Make a nest in the bushes just near that magnolia. You know the one."

Yes, she knew it well, and it wasn't only because she had sneaked a peek at the sketchbook he had been working on for weeks, entranced by the gorgeous watercolours of that exquisite creature. No, she recalled the tree from a long while ago. It was just a sapling then. This was the spot Joshua had brought Ingrid for a picnic, soon after it was planted. She had watched from the bushes then too.

My goodness. The back of Freddie's neck warmed as Joshua began speaking, soothing his subject into submission. This Isabella certainly was something, even better in the daylight. What she had seen from her hiding place the other evening was amazing yes, but all came as such a shock she could hardly focus. And then it was over too soon. But now, settled into her nest she had time to relax and enjoy every nuance. Freddie gazed at those breasts as they swelled over the top of the shawl, and watched the nipples harden as Joshua seduced her with his sex talk. She was mesmerized. Reaching a hand up to touch her temple, her silver bracelet slipped down her arm into the sunlight.

Freddie swore under her breath. She had been so careful to stay hidden in the shade and out of the wind to avoid being heard or seen. But she had forgotten to take off the bracelet. She'd have to be careful it didn't glint in the sun. She brought her arm down carefully and looked down at it, fiddling with the clasp.

The next thing she knew that beautiful face was peering at her through the undergrowth. She heard the sharp intake of breath.

"What? Who are … oh no, oh no, Joshua, I can't believe it …"

The voice stuttered, then broke into strangled, rasping sobs as the magnificent creature backed away from the bushes where Freddie was crouched.

Freddie unclenched her fist and the bracelet fell to the ground.

Isabella grabbed her shirt and coat with one hand, the other clasped the ends of the shawl together to cover herself. Ignoring Joshua's cry, she ran for the exit.

She ran, stumbling, towards the station, pausing only to pull on her shirt and coat behind a tree before leaving the gardens. She was oblivious to anyone around, running as if she were being chased by a wild animal.

Isabella stopped short when she reached the road, panting, waiting to cross. She heard a shout from behind her but did not look. It was probably Joshua, trying to coax her into coming back. As she reached the station, her pace slowed. She glanced quickly behind, but there was no one who looked like Joshua in the distance. She went through the barrier and waited numbly on the platform. Noticing that the next train was not for a few minutes, she took a quick side trip to the ladies' room to investigate the damage.

When she walked back onto the platform, there was a figure facing away from her standing tall, straight backed in the distance. A tilted felt fedora and black-belted raincoat, a black and silver striped scarf carefully knotted at the throat. An impressive look. She was briefly stunned. Confused. As if time had gone backwards. She had seen that stiff posture before. But surely not, it must be her imagination. As she angrily strode forwards, Isabella waited for Joshua to turn and greet her. But no. Here was Freddie herself. The gall! Not Joshua, not the lover come to apologize and seek forgiveness or attempt to reconcile … the wife!

"Yes, Isabella, it's me. No – don't go, don't turn away from me ... I have some things to say. I hope you will stay to hear them."

"My train is coming," Isabella said heatedly.

"Please."

"I must go," Isa almost spat the words, "back to Cambridge. Away. It's just too much."

She couldn't believe that Freddie was standing here, brazenly asking her to wait. What could she want to talk about? What did she think Isabella needed to know?

"Please," she repeated calmly. "Just a few minutes, a cup of tea, or a drink. You look like you need it. I shocked you – I'm sorry. You are quite pale. I can't have you travelling alone in this state. I don't want anything to happen to you."

Isabella tried to focus. Her head spun. She was dizzy, the urge to bolt so strong. She turned away but felt a hand on her shoulder. Not heavy or aggressive.

For some reason, she didn't shrug it off. The touch was firm but gentle, the fingers just brushing the skin of her neck.

She half turned, looking properly at Freddie for the first time. She saw a question, an invitation, in those deep brown eyes, and a serious but calm expression on the somehow plain but striking face.

They sat together at a table just outside the station café, Isabella hunched over her steaming tea.

Freddie calmly lit a long, black cigar. "I'm glad you stayed. There is so much I'm sure you've not been told. Joshua lets on very little. And all from his own point of view. Don't judge him too harshly; he is very scarred. He is an extraordinary talent. But that is really all he is."

"So ... have you come here to defend him? To plead on his behalf? Is he so weak? All he has done over and over is offer something, then pull it away. Be kind, then lie!" Isabella blurted out her words and sat straighter in her chair, lifting her chin. She curled her lip. "This is pathetic, ridiculous! I never should have agreed. My train is due – I'm going."

She rose from the table. Again, that gentle but firm hand stopped her, this time by the arm.

"No, please, finish your tea. Let me explain. I know. I'm aware of his draw. Of how he can pull you in. I've been there too. But I also know how he feels about you. And the impact that has on his work. There's a deep need in him for this intrigue. Perhaps in both of us. It may be the core of what has kept us together all these years. And now you've become part of it, willingly or not. You've become entwined with us."

The low tone matched the pressure on her arm. A kind but firm invitation to think again, to wait.

"But I don't want that. I want to get out, away from it all … You can play whatever games you like with each other. This is it for me. I'm setting myself free."

Freddie raised a perfectly shaped eyebrow. "But why? Haven't you enjoyed yourself? Maybe not all of it. I know he – we – have caused you pain. But the great heights, the delights, haven't they been worth it. No? Perhaps you need to stop and think about it. About why you've kept coming back to him. To us. You can't get to great passion unless you let yourself go. The intensity is essential.

"You can't just play around the edges."

As Freddie sat smoking her cigar, she may have seemed calm on the outside but inside, her gut was churning. *Never has anyone had quite this effect on me.*

There was a powerful, intense urge within her to not let this creature escape.

She had quickly recovered from the shock of seeing Isa's flushed face and flashing eyes glaring at her through the foliage. Freddie's long stride had given her the advantage; she'd known she could catch up.

It was time to play the sympathetic, compassionate friend. Even provide comfort that it wasn't Joshua who had come after her. Take the focus away from the fact that she was the conniving wife and reel her back in.

Isabella sank slowly back into her chair, mesmerized by Freddie's voice, but not exactly sure why. She was well aware that the best thing would be to leave, but part of her was caught like a rabbit in a trap. Part of her even wanted to be caught. This web of intrigue was so foreign to her, so beguiling. She felt lulled by the warm and steady tones of Freddie's voice. The woman's words washed over her, making that station table a brief haven after the turmoil of her escape from Kew, even though she'd been escaping Freddie herself.

But what was it exactly? What was it about the power of these two – were they the male and female version of the same thing? Perhaps they represented what she needed to resolve. The thing that kept cropping up through all those failed relationships. Maybe she needed to have it offered to her again and again so she could finally learn her lesson. Maybe, in the beginning of these affairs, it was as simple as needing adoration to heal the wounds of her past. To help erase the scars. But why did she then get scratched at again, wounded again, over, and over?

In that moment she had clarity. She would do what it took to work this through to a resolution. To get closure. She needed to take the time to learn, and heal, where the core lay to her own scarring. She would take the upper hand and never put herself in the victim position again.

Isa shook her head, her hair flying free. She breathed in deeply through her nose and forced herself to lower her shoulders, relax the tension.

Then she rose. "I really must go. The next train is due very soon."

The hesitation in her tone was gone, strength replacing it. She wouldn't waver this time.

Freddie raised a brow, but this time Isabella wasn't fooled. *You aren't so scary. I have the power here.*

She looked the woman directly in the eye and even gave her a brief smile before walking away.

"Goodbye."

Epilogue

There were two pieces of mail in her pigeonhole this morning. One was addressed in a characteristic, looped script she recognized immediately.

The only question was whether she would destroy it before or after she read it. Isa couldn't deny that she'd been wondering how he was, what had happened when Freddie returned to him in the gardens … whether the painting had been a great success. She had heard nothing from him, and it had been several weeks. But that had been the way she wanted it. He'd shown where his loyalties lay. And he hadn't been the one to follow her. She had been telling herself for weeks that she wanted no more of him.

All the way back in the train, she had played and replayed everything that had happened. Why had the Joshua and Freddie duo been such a hook for her? Perhaps she had found them at exactly the right time to help her move on. She still had some emotional work to do. But she was now in a much more powerful place. *Forewarned is forearmed* was another of her mother's sayings. It would stand her in good stead.

For now, Isa's research had provided all the distractions she needed. That was all coming along really well. The intrigues in her academic life she could manage. They were controllable, and there was plenty to keep her amused.

She caught sight of Simon across the quad, also coming to collect his mail. Isabella was still feeling badly about Simon. Did he think she blew hot and cold? They had not had any contact since that night she cried on his shoulder. A part of her knew she owed him an explanation. She promised herself she would at least give him that … but not right now. Right now, she was distracted by that second letter.

She turned it over in her hands. Coincidence that it arrived at the same time as the other? The script was confident, the print bold and commanding, on heavy, high-quality paper. The envelope was large, as if it contained several sheets. It was gilded at the corners. It was encircled with a ribbon, striped in black and silver and tied like a legal document. And there, on the envelope flap, were more black and silver stripes, and in silver ink:

you can't just play around the edges.

Very curious now, her heart pounding, she slit the back of it open.

It was a document. A proposal. An invitation to a contract negotiation where the duo seeking her partnership were prepared for her to set whatever terms she wanted. Their desire for her had an undertone of desperation.

Yes! She had the upper hand now.

Isabella needed to think long and hard about her next move…

ABOUT THE AUTHOR

A practicing therapist, mediator, and conflict resolution specialist, writing erotica is on the other side of the brain for Cristina. Author of academic and non-fiction titles, About Face is her first erotic novella. A sequel is in the works!

Cristina is an Australian native, who has made Canada her home. She is a mother, and grandmother.

She goes where the world and opportunities take her.